Sarah

I hope 1998 brings
you everything
you wish for!

Bob Boyd

MW00679622

His Father's Son

by

Robert W. Boyd III

DORRANCE PUBLISHING CO., INC.
PITTSBURGH, PENNSYLVANIA 15222

ISBN # 0-8059-4259-9
Printed in the United States of America
First Printing

For information or to order additional books, please write:
Dorrance Publishing Co., Inc.
643 Smithfield Street
Pittsburgh, Pennsylvania 15222
U.S.A.

Dedicated

to the memory of my father .....

Robert W. Boyd III

Chapter 1

He wasn't exactly unconscious. He didn't know when he became aware, or for that matter, that he had ever been unaware of his being. He was surrounded by, no he was part of, a rhythmic ebb and flow of colors with no beginning and no end. The colors were him, and he was part of the rhythm. There were no words, no music, no sound at all, but the gentle pulse of the rainbow that engulfed him was as an instrument, and he was the symphony.

It was a wonderful existence with no self, no ego, no demands, no sorrow, no fear, no expectations, no past, no future; it just was. There was no sensation of anything changing, but ever so slowly, like the movement of a glacier, an awareness of being had crept into the modulation. A sense of self, that had not been there before, began to form.

From the first hint of separation, there had been an overwhelming reluctance to disengage from the beauty and the timeless place that existed in the colors, but even more irresistible was the power of the self, that once apparent, became unstoppable.

The brilliance of the colors faded as the sentient mind increased its awareness. It was impossible to tell how long the process took. It could have been an eternity, or it could have been an instant. There was no way to tell, and in fact it made no difference.

When he awoke, the memory he had was of the colors. Where he was, who he was, how he got there, were questions that he would have to face at some time in the future. His first thoughts upon awakening, however, were regret that he was no longer in the world of colors. Somehow, he knew that he would never return to the rapture of unawareness from which he had come.

Chapter 2

Eva had been assigned as night nurse to the John Doe who had been brought into the hospital three weeks earlier. Discovered in the garage of an old hotel on the outskirts of town, at first the police thought he was a drunk who had passed out after a night on the town. However, when they could not rouse him, they brought him to the emergency room where after a battery of blood tests, it was determined that there was no indication of alcohol or drugs, and that he was in some sort of coma. Oddly the blood tests and all subsequent tests were negative and there was no sign of any illness or disorder. In fact, as Eva had noticed, this man was about as perfect a specimen as she had ever seen . . . and she had seen plenty, both on the job and off. As she cared for him, she became quite attached and attracted to him, taking great pains to make him comfortable, giving him sponge baths every night, turning him in his bed, and manipulating his arms and legs to maintain their flexibility.

Two things had occurred in the three weeks that he had been in the hospital that had surprised her. First of all, despite total inactivity, there seemed to be no loss in muscle tone or atrophy of the muscles themselves. Secondly, he was physically very attractive and clearly well-endowed, and she had begun to have sexual stirrings from the first moment that she saw him. She nevertheless had treated his body with the utmost respect. She longed to touch him as a woman would a man. Under different circumstances she would have, just to see how deep a coma he was in, and to observe how his body would react to certain caresses; but for some reason, in this case she restrained herself. There was something different about him . . . with him, she would wait.

Chapter 3

He was about 6'2", approximately 195 pounds, well muscled, no scars, tattoos or other unusual identifying marks. He appeared to be in his late 20's or possibly early 30's, had brown hair, a clear complexion and showed no signs of injury or foul play. He just wouldn't wake up.

The hotel owner had discovered the body wrapped in a clean white sheet in the garage, and at first had thought that it was dead. On closer inspection, it was apparent that the body was indeed alive, as it was breathing rhythmically. It was obvious, however, that something was wrong when despite his nudging, and pushing, and gentle whispers that quickly became verbal demands to wake up, the body just lay there, totally oblivious to the commotion going on around it.

When the police arrived, they quickly assumed this situation to be the aftermath of the DT's or a drug overdose and had called the Eden Prairie Ambulance Service to rush the John Doe to the hospital. Search as they might, they found no clue to his identification . . . no clothes, no wallet, no jewelry of any kind. The officers and the paramedics who had arrived with the ambulance all remarked that this was a first, and later when they learned that there was no indication of foul play, no evidence of drugs or alcohol, the circumstances became even more intriguing. Enough comment had been made that the next morning, the Sentinel ran a brief story in the human interest section, including a request by police for anyone who might have any information as to the identity of the mysterious stranger to please call it in.

There was, of course, no response, because in fact, no one in Eden Prairie or anywhere else for that matter had a clue as to who this gentlemen was . . . including himself.

Chapter 4

He became increasingly aware of his surroundings. He was in a small, but pleasant hospital room, designed as a double, but he was the sole occupant. His bed was closest to the door, away from the window as a convenience to the nurses and in recognition of the fact that an unconscious man cannot enjoy the view.

Although totally unaware of it, he had been poked, prodded and probed in every conceivable way. He had been subjected to an electroencephalogram, an electrocardiogram, a brain scan, x-rays, and then a full body scan in the MRI. A complete blood work-up followed by a second, even more thorough blood analysis after the first had come up with no unusual information. All results had been the same. They were not inconclusive. There was simply nothing wrong as far as modern medical technology could determine. The doctors had been very perplexed, so when Eva noticed that he seemed to be coming around, she immediately called the resident in charge of the case, who also happened to be on duty that night.

His eyes were now open, and he was following her graceful movements as Eva hurried about updating his chart for the doctors, taking his blood pressure and pulse, placing the reflex hammer on the bedside table and generally making preparations for the imminent arrival of the doctor. Eva was also watching him closely and carefully with a nurse's trained eye, looking for surprise, shock, confusion, disorientation or anything unusual. She was also aware of his eyes following her. Although she couldn't explain it, she felt a warmth and kinship with this stranger that had not existed when he was unconscious. She simply felt he knew her, yet she was absolutely positive that she had never seen him before. A man with a face and body like this one, she would remember!

Chapter 5

He was neither afraid nor confused. He was now fully awake and at peace with this new state. The world of colors was fading quickly, as does a pleasant dream that you want to remember, but can't quite. He was past the regret in leaving the living rainbow existence and was now drinking in the sights and sounds of his new environment. Like a newborn baby, it was too early in his awareness for him to be curious. His senses were overwhelmed by the most ordinary things: the movement of the door as the resident entered the room; the cold feel of the stethoscope as it touched his chest; the constriction of the blood pressure cuff; the change in light as a car passed below the window as the periphery of its beams briefly lit up the room. He noticed a faint, but pleasant aroma surrounding Eva, and a medicinal alcohol smell on the doctor as the resident thumped his chest, felt his neck glands and looked into his eyes, nose and ears. He was totally compliant and neither helped nor resisted in any way. While he understood the steady stream of questions that the doctor directed toward him, as well as the conversation between Eva and the doctor, he felt no need to respond. He just absorbed everything like an unquenchable thirst.

They had removed the IV and feeding tubes that had provided his sustenance over the past three weeks, and Eva had brought him a light broth. She sensed that he was perfectly capable of feeding himself, that he was aware and alert enough, as well as strong enough, but she wanted to do it, and delighted in the way that he seemed to savor every spoonful. She even thought she saw a grateful twinkle in his brilliant blue eyes, but he never said a word.

In the morning, there was no apparent change. He was awake and alert, but apparently unconcerned with his whereabouts or condition, or how he had come to be in the hospital, or how long he had been there.

It seemed that he was the only one who was not curious about the circumstances of his mysterious appearance in Eden Prairie. A police detective had been assigned to the case and the Sentinel continued monitoring his condition with an occasional follow-up blurb in the

5

daily paper.

Now that he was awake, both the detective and newspaperman were anxious to see him. In fact, they had been trading suppositions and theories in the waiting room until they finally received the doctor's approval to see him.

"I've never seen a case of total amnesia before. I just can't imagine that he can't remember anything . . . who he is, where he's from, the members of his family? For crying out loud, we don't even know if he speaks English or can even talk." The detective's thoughts were flowing into his conversation.

"Don't be so sure he has amnesia," said the reporter. "Maybe, he had some kind of stroke in his brain that the doctors couldn't find, and he has all kinds of thoughts and memories, but simply can't communicate anymore. I had an uncle like that. He had been a newsman for 35 years . . . brought me into the business. Then he had a stroke and became a basket case, couldn't utter a word. But, if you looked closely into his eyes when you talked to him, you just knew he could understand. He just couldn't respond. Sometimes the frustration in his eyes was terrible."

The cop looked skeptically back at the reporter. "Naw, I've read all the medical reports released by the hospital. They did every kind of test on this guy and there is nothing wrong with him. Definitely no stroke, they ruled that out very early."

Chapter 6

There indeed was no mental or physical impairment. There was no amnesia. He knew there was nothing wrong physically and his mind was functioning perfectly. Unlike the detective, reporter, doctors and nurses, he had no concern about who or where he was. Now that he was fully aware of himself, his first encounter with curiosity was, why?

Why was he here? What was he to do? He knew his existence had a reason and he believed that the reason would eventually make itself known. In the meantime he was content just to be and to absorb the reality that surrounded him.

The second night after his awakening, he lay in bed reflecting on the barrage of activity that was going on around him. He was amused at how the simplest activity on his part was considered "forward progress". When he got up on his own and went to the bathroom, you'd have thought he had invented the wheel or walked on water, the way the doctor and the day nurse had fussed and praised him. It was quite like the way you praise a puppy for learning a new trick, or a toddler for saying his first word.

His amusement was not cynical or disrespectful as he recognized the confusion about his "condition" by those attending him. He also recognized that their attitudes reflected a true concern for his well-being and "improvement". He was just not ready to become pro-active in the direction he was to follow. After all, since he didn't yet know why he was here, how could he possibly know what to do? So he watched them while they watched him. It was amusing.

Chapter 7

Eva, on the other hand, knew exactly what she wanted to do. She had been thinking about it ever since she woke up that afternoon, while she bathed, ate and dressed for the night shift. She even rationalized that what she was about to do would be therapeutic for him, and that perhaps it would snap him back into reality. She dressed in her regular nurses' uniform, but wore the scantiest of bikini briefs and her sexiest lace bra. She dabbed an extra touch of Tabu behind her ears, under her chin and just below her navel. With her peaches and cream complexion, she rarely wore makeup and tonight was no exception, but she did select the spicy red lipstick that she saved for special occasions. She knew that if she asked Martha, the other night nurse on the floor, to go out for pizza during her break, she would have at least 45 minutes that she could spend alone with him. Not very long, but certainly long enough for her to offer her own brand of recuperative therapy.

When Martha left for the pizza, Eva immediately checked the other patients on the floor. There were only nine others and they were all sleeping soundly.

Chapter 8

Eva had been born 27 years earlier on a small dairy farm outside of Eau Clair, Wisconsin. Her father was a hard-working farmer, and like many of his neighbors and friends, was of Swedish descent. He was very proud of his heritage, hard work and his successful dairy herd. Her mother was the daughter of German immigrants and was a statuesque blonde, blue-eyed beauty. Eva had come by her classic features and breathtaking good looks naturally, but one could only guess where her wild and passionate nature had come from. Both of her parents had been salt of the earth, hard-working folks who delighted in the fresh air, the early mornings and the pleasure in watching the fruits of their labor grow. The milk from their herd was like the lifeblood of their marriage, and they shared in the joy of watching the business prosper. They lived simple lives with few luxuries, plowing most of the profits back into the business, building new dairy barns, updating the milking machines and increasing the herd, always before they thought of upgrading their own standard of living.

Eva was altogether different. From her earliest recollection, she hated the farm. The beauty that her parents saw in the herd was lost to her in the stench that she never seemed to get away from. That they didn't seem to even notice, was incredible to her. It was everywhere! She felt the odor was permanently embedded in her clothes and in her hair. She tasted it when she ate her meals and she was embarrassed by it when she went to school. Her mother was pleased that Eva took such good care of herself, washing her hands before and after every meal, and bathing at least once, and often twice a day. What her mother didn't realize was that Eva's cleanliness and frequent bathing, were the result of an unnatural feeling of ever-present filth that Eva had built up in her mind as a result of the overwhelming smell of the dairy cows.

Like her parents, the other children that grew up on dairy farms and went to school with Eva, were unaware of her concern. They too had been raised within the pervasive smell of the dairy barns, but they, as their parents and Eva's parents, had become used to the fetor at an early age, and were not even aware of it.

Why she was different, she didn't know, but one thing she was sure of was that she would move away, "get away", from the farm as soon as she possibly could. When she mentioned this to her parents, they laughed and called her a dreamer. They fully expected that she would grow up, marry a local farm boy, and live and love the farm life just as they had.

Eva reached puberty at age 11 and appeared to be three or four years older than her actual age. While this concerned her parents somewhat, they were comforted by the fact that she seemed to have no interest in boys. She liked to play dress-up a lot and seemed particularly intrigued by her mother's perfume. Even though they knew that some of her girl friends were starting the early adolescent games that girls play with boys, they saw no evidence or indication of any interest on Eva's part.

The reality, however, was quite the contrary. Eva had been thinking about boys from the moment that her body had released the first female hormones that were reshaping her mind even faster than they were reforming her little girl body into the nubile nymph that she now saw in the mirror. She didn't understand these feelings, but she knew that she needed to keep them buried and completely hidden. When the other girls talked about boys, she did not participate. To her, their immature thoughts and desires were almost infantile. Their games of spin the bottle, "going steady", and constant gossip about boys bored her. She knew that she was ready for more and she knew that someday she would have it, but in the meantime, she knew that she had to keep the burgeoning longings deep within herself. Her parents would have never understood. Somehow, she knew that her drives and desires were far beyond those that most people ever experience. If she talked about her feelings, she knew that she would be regarded as a freak, frighten her parents and probably more importantly, she would have to admit them to herself. Something inside her told her that she must keep these yearnings, that she felt so strongly, but didn't understand, deep within herself. If she let them run free, there was no telling what would happen. For now, they were to remain buried.

10

Chapter 10

Special Agent Murray Greenbaum of the FBI had an unusual assignment. After 20 years with the Bureau, his ability to filter through detail for pertinent data, combined with his innate instinct for sniffing out the facts, had landed him a position on the Bureau's clipping service audit desk. The Bureau paid clipping services throughout the United States to cut out and send stories that might be pertinent to the FBI based on a list that covered over 2,000 topics ranging from common crimes to the unlikely, unusual and inexplicable.   AP and UPI stories were not included since they were wired directly into the Bureau, as were the foreign news releases from services such as TASS out of Russia.

Murray had a staff of 30 young agents who scanned the volumes of stories that came in daily. Anything that they found to be unusual or likely to be of interest to the brass, such as a crime pattern that had gone previously unnoticed, or an increase in organized crime, or even new union activity in an area, would be set aside for further review.   While ordinary citizens might question the value of this labor intensive and clearly subjective analysis of common everyday published information, Murray knew, as did his superiors at the Bureau, that properly trained agents had utilized this seemingly mundane service to detect and even help solve many crimes ranging from serial murders to major counterfeiting rings.   Although there were many dead ends, occasionally they were able to anticipate crimes and had saved property, even lives, as a result of this careful scrutiny of local news from a national perspective.

As patterns emerged, they were entered into the computer to be cross-indexed and correlated. Thus, it was generally a combination of human scanning and computer analysis that brought forth the results. Murray had been pushing   the   Bureau   to   install   new   sophisticated computerized scanning and sorting equipment that could eventually eliminate the need for the clipping services. He knew they could scan and automatically correlate any topics deemed important to the FBI.   The technology certainly was available and his superiors were verbally in favor of it, but somehow, his recommendations never made the cut when the final budget was submitted each year; too many dollars for a little recognized and less understood service.

Had the new technology been implemented, the story from Eden Prairie, Wisconsin would have never made it to his desk. It didn't correlate with anything. There was no apparent crime involved - no life threatening illness, in fact, no apparent illness at all. It was just one of those unusual stories that had caught the eye of one of his agents who had a hunch that it might be of significance. Murray had instilled in his young proteges that, in this business, instinct and hunches meant a lot. He encouraged them to "follow their nose", so to speak, and bring stories to him that seemed important even if they didn't really know why.

Chapter 11

John Doe was now up and about. He was eating normally and seemed to have had no difficulty in switching over from intravenous and feeding tubes to regular food. The doctors, at first, had been very careful, but it was obvious that his system had adjusted immediately. While his intake was limited to the bland foods available on the hospital patient menu, he was handling it just fine, and was clearly normal in his appetite, digestion and elimination. They were still monitoring everything from intake to stool weight, however, now it was more out of curiosity than to insure that they had not missed something. Indeed, he seemed to be as healthy a specimen as any one of them had seen.

Now that he was getting around, and there seemed to be nothing medically wrong with him, other than he had not spoken, written or communicated a single word since awakening, the business end of the hospital started to come around. Inquiries were made to the doctors as to how his identity could be determined, and how his stay was going to be paid for. He had, according to policy, been admitted with no question as an unconscious emergency John Doe, but now that he was diagnosed as free of any illness, he would soon be released and the hospital needed to be paid.

The doctors had determined from the condition of his skin, hair, teeth and nails, as well as his healthy vital signs, that prior to his appearance at the hospital, he had been eating and apparently living properly, as he suffered from no minor ailments or imperfections. They were, in fact, amazed to discover that he didn't have so much as dandruff or even a cavity. The were perplexed by his lack of communication. His eyes were bright and seemed to sparkle with understanding, yet he refused to try to communicate. No, refused was the wrong word. He simply didn't respond.

Chapter 12

Everyday he learned more about himself, about his surroundings, but more importantly to him, about those around him. He had learned that the first resident that had seen him in the emergency room and was still in charge of his case, was a warm and caring person. He was a young man who had gone to medical school for all the right reasons. He wanted to heal people. He wanted to help them. Money was incidental to him. His world revolved around doctor/patient relationships, and while many of his colleagues had found medical school, and the incredible hours spent as an intern, to be an endurance test to struggle through, he had enjoyed every minute of it.

John Doe listened carefully as the resident talked to him, asked him questions, and told him stories trying to evoke a response. As John listened, he learned a great deal more than the words themselves could convey. He began to know about this man, and, in the same way that you know something is about to happen, or you know how a movie will end, he knew this young man's feelings, and he liked what he saw in his mind. Strangely he didn't understand why or how he knew, nor did he recognize or realize the significance of this understanding. He just knew and it made him feel good.

His feelings regarding Eva were quite different. He had been totally unaware of her presence during the three weeks that she had cared for him while he was unconscious. Since awakening, however, he had become undeniably aware of her in the most intimate sense possible. It was the second night of awareness that she had come into his room. His eyes were closed, but he was fully awake and alert, and was immediately aware of her presence. He could hear her breathing and could smell the fragrance of her perfume mixed with the naturally pleasant aroma of her body. He listened without moving as he heard her remove her clothes and quietly place them on the empty bed by the bay window. Ever so gently, she climbed into bed next to him.

At first she just lay there as though contemplating her next move, or perhaps rethinking what she was about to do. Apparently, she pushed aside any second thoughts,

14

and ever so gently began to caress his neck. He was lying on his back, covered only by the hospital gown and sheet. She was lying close to him so that his relaxed extended right arm touched her body from neck to thigh. She had snuggled so close that her breasts had engulfed his upper arm and he could feel the mound of her pubic area touching the back of his hand. Although her caresses were feather-light, he sensed an overwhelming need within her, an emotional emptiness that had never been filled. He guessed that she had been with many men, and although it had been physically satisfying, it had never been enough. Her needs were deeper, and her previous attempts at quenching the fire within her had been totally unfulfilling, yet she knew no other way.

All these things he knew. He didn't know how or why he knew, he just did.

As she caressed his face, she ran her fingers over his lips and the second time she did so, he reached up with his left hand, caught her right hand in his, held it to his lips and gently kissed her. It was all the confirmation that she needed. She continued to caress his face as she leaned further over him and began kissing his neck with tender angel kisses. Her right hand had discovered that he indeed was fully excited and she was pleased with the obvious power of his response.

John knew that she needed him. He knew that he could and would be a part of her life, and that he could help her fill that empty void that had made her life to date so frustrating and unfulfilling. He also knew that sex with her was not the answer, and would be of little help to her, in fact he was sure it would be a hindrance. Yet he was, after all, a man he rationalized, and this Nordic classic beauty was kissing him with ever-increasing urgency. She was holding him and stroking him with a technique so expert that he was having trouble thinking of anything else. As she began to reposition her body directly over his, he gave in, or perhaps a better description would be that he joined in.

He stopped thinking and began responding. His left hand reached over and gently grasped her smooth rounded yet firm behind as he maneuvered her on top of him. For a few minutes, they teased each other as she arched above him kissing his neck and nipples, while he softly caressed her from top to bottom with his fingernails drawn up and down her spine. She could feel him brushing up against her, and she could stand it only so long before she reached down and guided him into her. Although their foreplay had aroused her tremendously and she was incredibly wet, he was large and strong and the initial thrust would have been painful had he not taken such care, despite his growing urgency, to enter her very slowly and deliberately with a series of small thrusts each gently and slowly going deeper than the last.

As he entered her, the thought hit her through the swirling whirlpool of emotions that this was the most incredible man that she had ever met, and she didn't even know his name or where he came from. Far from concerned about this lack of information, she was caught up in the moment and her mind quickly abandoned any thoughts of who or why, as she was totally consumed by the physical sensations that she was now experiencing.

This man was everything she had ever dreamed of and more. She could feel the strength of his body as his arms encircled her and his back arched with every stroke. His strength more than surrounded her, it was more than in her. His strength was more than physical, it seemed to come from within and surround him like an aura. In this moment of sexual unity, she felt that somehow she was sharing his strength, a power that she sensed went way beyond the physical. She didn't know how, but she could tell that he knew better than she did of her wants and needs. He knew about the emptiness, the loneliness, the fears. He knew about the past. He had known that she was going to come to his bed and in this moment of rapturous enlightenment and unity, she realized that he also knew her future and yet she was not surprised. All these things she felt and knew at once. Perhaps the words weren't there in her mind, but the thoughts were there. Furthermore, she was aware that she would never be the same again.

He too had become lost in the physical act, and overwhelmed by the sensuous responses of this beautiful woman. He also knew that he would be there for her, help her to fill the void, end the loneliness, end the fear. He knew her past and he foresaw her future; and he knew that their lives would be forever linked.

16

She felt the waves of a magnificent orgasm surging through her body. She felt him climax and as their bodies rhythmically joined together, she felt each joyous spasm surging from him to her as an electric current that sent shocks of almost unendurable pleasure throughout her body.

As he relaxed from the last wondrous convulsion, he knew that this was the most perfect physical experience that two human beings could have together. He also realized that this would be the last time that he would ever make love with Eva or anyone else. While he still didn't know the purpose of his existence, he knew that this would only complicate matters, and this was not the way. This experience had momentarily helped Eva forget her emptiness, but he knew that it would be only a matter of hours, perhaps minutes, before she returned to reality and realized that nothing had been solved, nothing accomplished other than another experience with another man. He knew that he could do more, much more, for Eva and others. Sex would be a great temptation, almost irresistible, but he recognized that his focus must be on something more important. His last thoughts as he drifted off to sleep were, for now, he must figure out why he was here. He felt he was getting closer to an answer.

Eva gently kissed his sleeping body as she slipped out of bed. Little did she realized that the past 45 minutes of ecstasy would change her life completely and forever.

Chapter 13

Special Agent Murray Greenbaum read the article over and over. It was a small clip from the Eden Prairie Sentinel, a small newspaper from a small town in Wisconsin. He flipped through the brief follow-up stories and read again and again the strange circumstances surrounding the discovery of the unusual man, his three week coma and almost miraculous recovery. The fact that he was apparently healthy, seemingly intelligent, but wholly unresponsive, was the most intriguing aspect of the entire story.

Murray couldn't put his finger on it, but he had a gut feeling that this time they had stumbled on to something important, but he had no idea what. He had faxed an FBI query to the local police asking for all available information including police reports, medical records, fingerprints, etc. and had sent two local agents to snoop around. They weren't his men, of course, but at this point, he wasn't ready to spend any of his discretionary money on this project unless it were to develop into something.

Everything had come up blank. There was simply no background information on this man.

The hospital records were clear. They had no explanation for the coma, no explanation for the recovery, no evidence of illness of any kind. Similarly the Bureau drew a blank with the fingerprint search. The most thorough questioning from various professionals including psychiatrists, medical doctors, police detectives, and newspaper reporters, had all resulted in exactly the same response. He appeared to understand the questions, but in every session, he simply would not, or could not respond with any form of communication other than a warm smile. It was as though he were waiting for something.

Murray noted that several of the interviewers had commented on the apparent intelligence seen in his sparkling blue eyes. Looking into those eyes, they could tell that he understood and therefore they were all the more perplexed as to why he was so totally unresponsive.

Murray was amused that the hospital administrator

was becoming very agitated over the fact that, since the John Doe had no family or relatives, no friends of any kind, no job or even address, the hospital had no way to collect the bill that was mounting daily. The administrator was even more frustrated by the fact that they were having difficulty with the state bureaucracy in having him declared a ward of the state. Since he had no birth certificate, no driver's license, no social security number and no apparent plans or desire to identify himself, the state in all its wisdom, refused to recognize his existence. Meanwhile, the hospital doctors' committee was reluctant to transfer him to a mental hospital, and even if they did make such a recommendation, the administrator doubted that they could find any institution willing to take him due to his combined lack of identity, lack of solvency and the lack of any evidence of a mental disorder other than his persistent inability or perhaps unwillingness to engage in verbal communication.

Murray recognized that the enigma faced by the hospital represented something unusual, and probably important. He just couldn't figure out what it was!

Chapter 14

The hospital administrator was at his wit's end. There seemed to be no solution to this John Doe dilemma. The bill was adding up and the Board of Directors, who normally disregarded the daily operations of the hospital, was on his case to come to some sort of resolution. John Doe had now been at the hospital for six weeks. Everyone, including the administrator (although he was reluctant to admit it), liked him. He had a magnetic warmth about him that naturally drew people in. But who was going to pay the bill and what in the world were they going to do? This couldn't be allowed to go on indefinitely!

No one could have been more surprised than the hospital administrator when, one evening approximately seven weeks after he had arrived at the hospital, John Doe appeared at his office door dressed in hospital greens and slippers. He looked in and said, "It's time for me to go . . . thank you for everything."

John turned and left. The administrator was so stunned that he sat there in silence for a few moments before getting up to follow John down the hall. When he reached and opened his office door, perhaps a minute had passed since John's incredible first communication, and as the administrator looked in both directions, he quickly realized that John had disappeared from sight.

It didn't take very long to discover that John had not only disappeared from the hall, but apparently he had disappeared from the hospital as well. A thorough search of the building, and then the grounds, gave no clue to his whereabouts.

Characteristically, other than his brief surprise notice of departure to the stunned administrator, there had been no other communication whatsoever.

Chapter 15

Eva had gone through High School an enigma to the male student body. She was clearly the most beautiful girl in school with a sexy way about her that seemed to reflect an inner desire that appeared to be ready to break loose, but she was totally under control. Most of the boys thought of her as a tease because she "walked the walk", but to their disappointment, didn't "talk the talk" or in any way follow through in her actions what her appearance seemed to show. Much as many of the boys would have liked to crack that impenetrable barrier, they soon realized that her "forbidden fruit", while obviously ripe and ready, was not available to them.

The other girls had realized early on that Eva was in a league of her own looks-wise, and might have been extremely jealous, had it not been obvious that something above Eva was different. She refused to share any of her inner thoughts about boys and was always cool and aloof when the subject came up. On the other hand, she was not shy about her body and the other girls thought that she liked to take every opportunity to show it off, always taking the longest showers after gym class.

Eva was very confused. Nothing she heard at home from her mother regarding sex had even come close to her feelings. Her mother had provided a normal descriptive account of the changes she was experiencing as she entered puberty. She had helped her through her first period, which gratefully had come on a Saturday morning early, unlike some of her friends who had been mortified to discover that their first period had chosen to find them in school, totally unprepared and unaware, causing them no end of embarrassment as they rushed out of class to the nurse's office.

Her mother had also described sexual intercourse, both from a mechanical and an interpersonal standpoint, as the culmination of love between two adults. In health class, and again in biology, she had learned every last detail regarding sex, reproduction, parenting and all that went with it as part of the Wisconsin state-required curriculum.

At church and in Sunday school, although the

21

subject was never broached head on, she certainly was led to understand that "good girls" waited until they were married; that God had forbidden sex outside of marriage, and that those girls who had sex prior to or outside of the sanctity of marriage were "bad".

None of the mother-daughter talks, or classes in school, or church sermons, however, prepared her, or even seemed to have anything to do with her relationship to sex. For Eva, it was something she lived with. It was always there. Riding a bike, or sitting on a horse, feeling the warmth and massive strength of the animal beneath her, were almost too much for her to bear. Sometimes in the bathtub, or in bed late at night, when she touched herself and turned her raging desire into blazing ecstasy, she, for a few fleeting seconds would forget the shame for her loss of control as she lost herself in all-consuming waves of orgasm upon orgasm. When she finally finished, guilt and regret would settle in almost immediately. She always felt dirty, and even worse, despite the physical pleasure, she always felt unfulfilled.

In those early days, she knew, or thought she knew, that her lack of a sense of total fulfillment was a result of the lack of a man's involvement. Only later would she learn, much to her dismay, that while men sometimes made the experience slightly more pleasurable, eliminating the need to stimulate herself, she would find that she still would have the identical feeling of shame and emptiness afterwards.

Chapter 16

John remembered nothing about his existence prior to what he had come to think of as the world of colors. Yet, he was well educated and seemed to know a great deal about a great number of things. He did not question this knowledge, nor did he question his apparently unique ability to see and know things about people that his common sense told him he could have no way of knowing. To him, this extra sense was as natural as is hearing or sight to most people. If asked, he could not describe it. He did not read minds, or have telepathic powers, he simply knew things and every day the depth of this knowledge grew. Oddly enough, although he had just spent seven weeks in the hospital with virtually everyone from doctors to newsmen, to the FBI worrying and wondering about him, he himself was not in the least bit worried. Although he had no idea where he was going, how he would get there, or for that matter, where his next meal was coming from, he did not concern himself with these things.

It was as if his "self" were hidden safe and secure in the center of a large ball of yarn. As the ball would be batted this way and that, the center would be protected until the ball completely unraveled, and the center would finally be brought to light. In the meantime, he seemed perfectly content to go in whatever direction providence led him. Or perhaps better said, in whatever direction his inner silent voice had led him. For just as he couldn't explain why he had stayed in the hospital so long, he couldn't explain why he had abruptly left. He simply knew it was time for him to go and he accepted without question, that there was some reason that he had been in the hospital for that time.

Almost immediately after John walked out the front door of the hospital, an officer in a police car on routine patrol saw him. The officer, seeing the hospital greens and quickly noticing the green slippers, assumed that John was a doctor who had stepped outside for a breath of fresh air. He was in no particular hurry and had no calls to respond to, so he pulled over to chat. He knew most of the doctors in the area, having been a patrol officer in Eden Prairie for almost 20 years, but he didn't recognize this one.   He certainly would have remembered this handsome young fellow with such an athletic build.

Officer Duggan pulled over to the curb by John. He stopped the squad car, left the radio on and the engine running out of longtime habit, opened the door and said, "Hi doc, I don't think I've seen you around here before." Officer Duggan had heard the stories about John, but he never particularly paid attention to them. He clearly had no inkling that this man on the curb was anyone but a young doctor, perhaps an intern, new to the hospital.

"I don't believe that we've ever met", John replied. "I'm not ...". but before John could continue the sentence, the radio crackled and interrupted the moment.

"Officer down!   I repeat, officer down!   All units respond.   There's been a multi-vehicle accident at Route 202 and the Turnpike off-ramp. Shots have been fired and one officer is a probable fatality, another critically wounded.   There are two suspects on the scene.   They should be considered armed and dangerous. Please proceed with extreme caution." The dispatcher began to repeat the message.

Officer Duggan, previously casual, relaxed and calm, was now all business.

"Get in doc. There's no telling what we're going to find when we get there, but I'm sure we'll be able to use your help."

John didn't question. He jumped into the cruiser and as Officer Duggan hit the lights and siren, John began to feel the reappearance of the world of colors. This time he knew that he would not disappear into the rhythm. This time he sensed that it was a part of him that was there, just as much as his heart, or his mind, but it was hidden below the surface beyond his or anyone else's awareness.

As with many other things, John did not question the inner reappearance of the colors, but he was glad they were there. It was comforting to know that they were a part of him, or that he was a part of them.

John and the officer were not the first two to appear on the scene. Several other officers had arrived sooner and had apprehended a Latin-looking truck driver and his swarthy compadre. The truck had apparently exited the Turnpike at a high rate of speed. While it had negotiated the curved exit without mishap, the driver had failed to

24

apply the air brakes in sufficient time to stop at the end of the exit. The big rig had plowed into oncoming traffic. Miraculously, no one had been injured in the crash, which had almost totaled a Dodge Caravan and had done significant damage to a police car that had been passing by.

Once the two officers in the police car had determined that no one had been hurt in the Caravan, they had approached the cab of the truck. Apparently the driver and his companion had been hopped up on uppers or some other drug and for some reason, known only to them, opened fire on the two officers, emptying both barrels of a ten gauge shotgun in the process.

The officer closest to the truck took the brunt of the spray and went down immediately. The second officer, although hit in the face, chest and stomach, had managed to get back to the police car and radio for assistance before collapsing.

The first policemen arriving at the scene saw their brother officers down and called in the severity of the situation, asking for ambulances and backups. As it turned out, backups weren't necessary as the two Latinos seemed confused and bewildered by their own actions. They had jumped down from the truck and were standing over the first fallen officer, the driver holding the empty shotgun in his hands. They offered no further resistance when they were cuffed.

All of this was related to Officer Duggan by one of the young cops on the scene. Duggan wondered where the hell the ambulance was and was thankful for the stroke of luck that had brought a doctor to him at a time when one was so desperately needed.

John took it all in. He could see that while the one officer had multiple flesh wounds, and that he would have to have the shot removed, he could tell that the man was okay and that no vital organs had been damaged. The man was sitting on the ground, smoking a cigarette and talking coherently with the other officers as they waited for the ambulance. John instinctively knew that it was the first officer that needed him. He had no understanding or comprehension of what was about to happen, nor did he know how or why. He didn't think or question. He just acted.

He walked over to the officer on the ground, saw no movement, felt no pulse and knew the man was dead. Suddenly he felt the rhythm of colors grow within him, and for a moment, as he reached out and touched the officer's hand, he felt he was back in the timeless beauty of the soundless symphony, and for an instant, he drew the officer in with him. Together their souls embraced with an overpowering love that was beyond all understanding. Then it was over.

The officers watching saw no more than John bending down and touching the dead officer. As he rose, they assumed that there was no hope, that there was nothing that the doctor could do. Just then, the harsh blinking lights of the ambulance, together with the roar of the siren, broke the mood and a new flurry of activity started as the paramedics jumped out of the ambulance and ran to each of the fallen men. Looking quickly at both of them, they immediately began to work on the second officer, attaching an IV and giving him first aid as they loaded him into the ambulance.

Referring to the first officer downed, one of the paramedics said, "Get him some blankets and loosen his clothing. He's in shock." With that, the hitherto assumed dead man sat up and looked around.

Amazed and astounded, the police looked around for John, for an explanation, but he was nowhere to be found.

Chapter 17

He now knew who he was, and more importantly, why he was here.

Chapter 18

It took a little while for the Eden Prairie police to piece together the facts, but when they finally concluded that the "doctor" Officer Duggan had picked up was really the mysterious John Doe that had disappeared from the hospital, they were truly in a quandary. On top of that, the officer who had been shot with the shotgun at point blank range in front of witnesses, had not only fully recovered, but upon examination at the hospital, appeared never to have been shot at all. There were no wounds, no scars, no evidence whatsoever that he had been shot. Neither officer who had been wounded, nor the driver of the truck, who openly admitted to the shooting, could believe that the officer was not dead, much less appeared uninjured in any way. Even the blood which had spurted from his wounds, staining his shirt and puddling underneath his body had disappeared without a trace. His uniform was another matter. It was torn and full of holes just as one might expect after being shot at close range.

Had this event occurred in New York, Chicago, L.A. or any other major city, there is no doubt it would have created a media circus with the tabloids jumping all over it. In Eden Prairie, however, it raised eyebrows, caused confusion among the police, attending paramedics and hospital staff; but only resulted in a curious but brief article in the local paper.

ILLEGAL ALIENS STEAL TRUCK SHOOT OFFICER
"In a flurry of excitement uncharacteristic of Eden Prairie, police officers apprehended two illegal Mexican immigrants who, while apparently driving under the influence of drugs, collided with a police car and another vehicle at the Eden Prairie turnpike exit. Uninjured in the accident, the two officers in the police car were fired upon at point blank range by the driver of the truck, Alfonzo Lopez. One of the officers was hit and is in satisfactory condition at Eden Prairie General. The other officer was miraculously uninjured, but understandably in shock, and is being held for

28

observation. Lopez and his companion, Arturo Ramirez, were apprehended without further resistance when additional officers arrived on the scene. Inexplicably, John Doe, a recent amnesia victim recuperating at Eden Prairie General assisted the downed officers at the scene, but disappeared shortly after paramedics arrived. We don't know who you are, but Eden Prairie thanks you, and wishes you the best of luck wherever and whoever you may be !"

No one else in Eden Prairie thought very much about the article. It was not picked up by the wire services, and being a conservative and homey sort of family newspaper, it had omitted the strange and conflicting reports regarding the officer who had been shot at point blank range, but had sustained no injuries. The editors had also chosen not to play up John Doe's participation too much, although the rumors running through the police department were that witnesses claimed this man had actually healed the wounds of the officer, and perhaps even brought him back to life.

Since all of this was totally unsubstantiated by evidence, there were no before and after photographs, and no doctor had made an examination prior to John Doe having touched the man, the newspaper had been reluctant to publish what the editor had characterized as "crazy talk".

"Remember," he told his reporters, "two people witnessing exactly the same events can come away with entirely different versions of what happened. Everyone involved here was under extreme duress. They were keyed up and probably scared to death. No wonder they have come up with this crazy story. No one will ever know exactly what happened, but one thing you can be sure of, John Doe didn't bring a dead policeman back to life or heal point blank shotgun wounds. That just didn't happen!"

Chapter 19

When the brief article from Eden Prairie crossed Murray Greenbaum's desk with the lines regarding John Doe highlighted, it piqued his interest, reminding him of the earlier articles that had caught his attention, and the mystery about this man that was as yet unresolved.

It was late in the day, so he pulled out his file and placed it in the middle of his desk on his way out the door as a reminder to himself. First thing in the morning, he wanted to follow up with the agent that had been on the scene and determine if there was any reason to continue the investigation. Murray's gut told him that this particular John Doe would lead them in some very interesting directions.

Chapter 20

When John Doe realized that he had revived the officer, he also knew that he was not prepared to face the questions that were sure to come. So, in the mass confusion of the moment, he was able to slip away and run up the embankment onto the turnpike. He walked for a minute as cars and huge trucks whizzed by.

"I need to go somewhere to be alone and to think." His mind was going a mile a minute and he had to escape from people for awhile to settle his thoughts and formulate a plan.

"Where will I go? How will I get there?" He thought as a new eighteen wheeler pulling a shiny silver trailer with Muirfield Trucking written on the side approached through the night. Without thinking, he held out his hand as a sign to the driver to stop. As if by command, the driver hit the air brakes and the great truck came to a lumbering halt. John had to run about 100 yards to reach where the truck had finally come to a stop. As he approached the cab, the driver reached over, lifted the handle and pushed the door open.

"Climb aboard. You could have gotten yourself killed out here on the open highway. I can't imagine how I ever even saw you with those green, (what are they pajamas?) clothes on. Man are you lucky I came along. Where are you headed?"

Before John had a chance to answer, the driver continued, "Name's Paul, Paul Simons and I'm headed for Vegas. I've got a load of meat for one of those wholesale distributors that service all the hotels and restaurants. I don't know how far you're goin', but I'll enjoy the company . . . gets kinda lonely out here on the road."

"Just call me Chris," John said, "Chris Lambert". His eyes twinkled as he enjoyed the joke that only he could understand. "I guess I'm in luck because I'm headed West myself. I thought I could use a little time in the desert to sort things out and kind of get my life and priorities in order. I sure would appreciate it if I could ride with you all the way to Nevada. I think some time in the desert would be good for me."

"Are you kidding? As I said before, I'd love the

company. It's against regulations, but who's gonna tell? It looks to me as though we're gonna get to know each other real well in the next few days. I expect we'll hit Vegas in about four days." Paul went on, "Don't you have a bag or suitcase or anything? What are those clothes you're wearing, some kind of uniform or what?"

Chris looked at the driver. He was a big man with an expression as open and honest as the day was long. Obviously lonely from too many hours on the road, he appeared to have a good heart and sincerely welcomed Chris' company. All the questions and rapid-fire conversation were not disconcerting to Chris. This young man was a man of the people. A friend to everyone, including strangers. Chris read Paul as a good man, and a man with a purpose. He suspected that once Paul had made a decision, he would not deviate. Just as he pointed the big rig west and drove, once an idea was embedded in this man's mind, like a seed planted in fertile soil, it would grow straight and strong reaching for the sun, not to be swayed by wind or storm, rather to be strengthened by adversity.

In the first minute of conversation, Chris knew that Paul would be with him. He would be the first of many, and it was more than fate, it was providence that brought Paul down the turnpike at the very moment that Chris needed him.

As they rode, Paul told his story. Born and raised in a working class family in western Pennsylvania, he had always been big for his age and was outstanding in sports. While his interest in academics was less than his teachers would have liked, he was a smart kid and his intelligence displayed itself in many ways. He was not only physically adept at sports, but he understood sports. He was always surprising his coaches with new plays on the football field, designed on the spot, to most effectively impact the weak spots of the opposing teams.

In baseball, he understood the complexity and finesse of the game, frequently suggesting strategies to the coach that baffled the opposition; laying down unexpected bunts, stealing bases, bringing the infield in, or shifting the outfield based on his memory of each hitter's propensity.

Outside of sports and school, he had become

somewhat of a legend because of his ability to take a position and argue a point clearly, with conviction. He was not afraid to disagree or debate with anyone. Much to his parents' dismay, he was always getting into debates with his Sunday school teachers and later with the minister at their church.

"If God loves everyone, why do some people die horrible deaths? Why do we die at all? Why are some bad people very rich and some very good people poor?" His questions were penetrating and thoughtful beyond his years. He was very persuasive and he confounded the Sunday school teachers and even the minister himself. They not only couldn't reach him, they saw that he was persuading many of the other children to question the very fundamental beliefs of the church.

Paul had the unique distinction of being the only student in the local church's history to have completed eighth grade confirmation class, but not be confirmed by the church. Far from worrying him, he saw no reason to be confirmed and questioned his friends unmercifully about how hypocritical it was for them to be confirmed if they didn't truly believe; and how could they believe, or what kind of religion was it if they couldn't answer his questions? He wouldn't accept such answers as, "God works in mysterious ways"; or "accepting God enables you to make the 'great leap to faith'" without specific proof. He characterized these answers as weak rationalizations devised by the church, when in fact, they had no answers at all for the type of profound questions that constantly popped into his head.

His parents, especially his father, were very proud of his athletic prowess, considered his lukewarm interest in school work normal for a boy, but were quite concerned by what they considered a negative and disruptive attitude toward church and religion. They believed his attitude reflected badly on them and it hurt their standing among their friends and neighbors.

"Where have we gone wrong?" they would ask themselves, and "What have we done to deserve this type of disrespect?" they would ask Paul.

Paul would shrug and say, "I just don't believe all this stuff. You didn't do anything wrong."

They would just shake their heads, and hope or

perhaps rationalize that this was just a phase that their son was going through. They prayed that sooner or later his background and upbringing would catch up with him and he would "see the light".

After graduation from high school, Paul went to Penn State for one year. His talent for football had enabled him to receive a scholarship despite his mediocre grades. To this very day, he was glad that he had the opportunity to go to college, if only briefly, not because of the classes or professors, but because of the late night "bull sessions" in the dorm.

They discussed everything from politics to religion and, as freshmen do, they solved the problems of the world. This was the freshest outlet that he ever had for his ideas and he thoroughly enjoyed the open spirit with which different points of view were discussed.

Unfortunately, Paul failed to show the same zeal for his classes. Much to the disappointment of his parents and the football coach, he flunked out without ever having the opportunity to develop his football talents. His parents had been overjoyed when he went on to college, but they were distraught when he explained that he wouldn't be going back after his freshman year. After all, he was the first one in the family's history who had gone on even for one year after high school.

Paul lived at home briefly, but both his parents and he agreed that since he was out of school and working, it was time to get his own place. He worked construction for a while and became fairly handy with a hammer, but shied away from the trade unions. He just couldn't see the advantage and didn't want to pay the dues. The unions controlled the best jobs and soon he tired of taking leftovers.

He tried, what he euphemistically called the restaurant business, working for awhile as an assistant manager at a Bob Evans; but that work just didn't suit him. He wasn't very good at taking direction from people that he felt were like robots following stupid policy manuals that often didn't fit the individual circumstance and didn't make sense.

When Paul turned 21, he had had seven different jobs since high school and had yet to find himself. He had gone out with a number of girls, but had not become deeply attached or involved with anyone. His father had come up with an idea that his mother was concerned about, but as usual went along with. As a surprise for his 21st birthday, his father presented him with a used, but almost new, tractor trailer. It was a three-year old Peterbilt and was clean as a whistle.

Where his father found the insight to come up with the idea, Paul didn't know. He had never even thought of the possibility of driving a truck for a living, but the moment he saw the big eighteen wheeler, he knew that was just what he wanted to do. He had no ties other than his folks, and, being on the road, he would be able to see them pretty much whenever he wanted. He was amazed that his father had the money to buy the rig and it wasn't until a few years later that he learned that his parents had remortgaged their "paid for" home to provide him with this opportunity.

He was on top of the world. How many 21 year old guys owned their own truck? This was a business and a lifestyle without rules. He considered himself a free spirit, like one of the old-time cowboys who rode the range answering to no one. The solitude of the truck was lonely at times, but it gave his creative mind a chance to think. It had one impact on him that he was not really aware of, he missed the give and take of conversations. So, whenever he was at a truck stop, he always joined whatever group of truckers happened to be around and engaged them in conversation.

By the time he had been on the road for four years, he was known by his fellow truckers as the Talker, and had even picked it up as his handle on the CB. Strange as it may sound, he found that many of the late night discussions with other truckers reminded him of the dorm "bull sessions" that he had participated in during his less than fruitful, freshman year at college. To be sure, the crowd was older and definitely rougher around the edges. Perhaps they were a little more hardened or opinionated by the knocks that they had taken, but the topics were the same, politics to religion.

Once again, Paul found himself arguing the same arguments that he had begun in Sunday school, had continued in college, and was now expressing in truck stops, weigh stations and cheap motels around the country.

While the opposition had changed somewhat in personality, the arguments were pretty much the same:

"If there is no God, why are we here?

"Does existence make sense if 'being' ends with death?

"How can the 'miracle' of life be explained any other way than the existence of God?

"Aren't the concepts of right, wrong, guilt, shame, forgiveness, ethics, morality and prayer all based on a fundamental belief in a being greater than oneself?"

Paul's responses were simple and direct as they always had been. "We're here because we're here. Without proof of His existence, there is no God.

"An ephemeral existence makes as much sense as an eternal existence. Why not? Who says that life, being, or existence of any kind should be everlasting. Or better, what proof is there? None.

"Life is not a miracle . . . it just is. We just happen to be alive at this moment. There is no greater meaning. Belief that there is more is simply a natural human rationalization to ease the fear of the unknown.

"Right, wrong, guilt, shame, forgiveness, ethics, morality and prayer are all concepts evolved by man over many years of trial and error. Each of them had a basis in efficient use of time and energy, rationalizations regarding previous or planned behavior, or thought processes designed to alleviate individual or mass concern about the unknown."

Paul argued, "there was no 'greater good' nor ultimate right or wrong." These were just concepts developed by men in order for society to prosper. In effect, these high concepts were simply a part of the natural expediency of man in finding the shortest path to his ultimate goal, which was happiness; happiness in this life, the only life as far as he could tell.

Paul believed that the whole concept of God and the many religions that had sprung up around the world, were truly helpful and supportive to those who believed in them, but Paul inwardly held these "true believers" in contempt. Where was the proof? Where was the logic? Where was the evidence?

He dismissed the Bible as a collection of fiction assembled over a period of time to support a particular point of view. His favorite contemporary analogy compared the Bible to Madison Avenue and the advertising business. Who could disagree that with a combination of facts, figures and creative copy, the gurus on Madison Avenue could make anything look good. Paul's position was that the Israelites had done the same thing selling their beliefs as did the Christians later on.

Chris listened intently as Paul talked. "This man was truly the salt of the Earth," thought Chris. Although considerably misdirected, he was convincing and in his own way, he was a true believer. The more Chris heard, the more he was certain that Paul would play an important role in the future, although he wasn't exactly sure what that role might be. In the meantime, they had a long trip ahead of them during which he would gently begin Paul's education.

Chris smiled inwardly as he contemplated those soon to be held conversations.

They had been on the road for two days, just driving and talking when their conversation was abruptly interrupted.

"Oh, oh! See that red warning light on the dash?" said Paul. "That means something's wrong with the reefer."

He was hauling meat in a refrigerated trailer, and the worst thing that could happen, short of an accident was for the temperature in the trailer to go up. Even at night the meat could spoil in less than six hours, and in the direct summer sun, the meat would spoil in less than two hours if the refrigeration unit wasn't working.

Paul pulled over, got out and checked the trailer.

"Shit! The compressor's broke and we're two hundred and fifty miles of Idaho desert to the nearest truck stop that can replace it."

Paul had a look of anguish on his face. This was the first time anything like that had happened since he had become an independent contract carrier for Muirfield Trucking and Wilson Meats out of Monmouth, Illinois. He prided himself on his mechanical ability, and most of the time between his skills, the tools that he carried with him and spare parts, he could take care of any breakdown on the road. A compressor was different! Like the water heater in a home, it seemed to have a long and useful life, but when they were shot, it was serious and the only solution was replacement. The middle of the desert was not the place to lose a compressor.

Paul was perplexed. Not only were they out in the middle of nowhere, but the other truckers he radioed on the CB had confirmed his worst fear. Although there were a few cafes, motels and gas stations, there was no place to even have the reefer looked at for two hundred and fifty miles in either direction. Other independent truckers had told him that he should get insurance to cover this type of mishap, but Paul was young and optimistic. Every time the subject came up, he decided to save the money. Now, much as he hated to, he realized he better get to a phone and pass the bad news along to his dispatcher. Nobody was going to be happy about this!

As Chris listened to Paul explain the situation, he could feel the torment that Paul was experiencing. Here was a good man, working hard, doing his very best and now he had a financial disaster on his hands, with no way out.

"Paul, would you mind if I take a look before we find a phone?"

Chris surprised Paul. Paul could tell that Chris was smart, but he never even suspected that Chris might be able to help in this situation. His demeanor was that of a gentle, educated, thoughtful person, certainly not a mechanic.

"Chris, do you know anything about refrigeration or compressors?"

"Not really, but why not let me take a look anyway. It can't hurt."

Paul shrugged. After all, the compressor was already kaput. The meat was as good as spoiled. What difference would a couple more minutes make. At this point Paul was resigned to the situation. He accepted this disaster as his fate and just leaned back in his seat with his eyes closed as Chris went back behind the cab to look at the malfunctioning trailer.

Chris had only been out of sight for a moment when Paul felt a sensation that he had never felt before. Although he had never experienced it, he recognized and welcomed it. He knew he was in the desert alone with Chris and a truckload of meat, but suddenly, out of

38

nowhere, he had the sensation of being at the center, or very near to the center, of a power that he didn't understand, but totally accepted on an emotional level. He opened his eyes and emanating from behind the cab was a pulsating rainbow of colors. One instant it was there; the next it was gone. He sensed that if the colors had remained, he would have been drawn to them with an intensity he could only imagine as ten thousand times more powerful than that of a moth to a flame. Yet, he had seen only the briefest glimpse of the periphery of the colors whose center was located somewhere directly behind the cab.

Paul opened the door and leapt to the ground. He swung around behind the tractor and saw Chris climbing down from the hitch.

"The compressor seems to be working okay now," said Chris in his quiet understated way.

After several checks and repeated astonished glances at Chris, Paul was willing to accept that the compressor was indeed, once again, operational.

Paul looked at Chris. "How?" he asked.

Chapter 21

This wasn't the first time that Chris had surprised Paul, but there was no doubt it was the most startling, dramatic, and yes, even miraculous. It made Paul think back to something that had happened shortly after he had picked Chris up on the highway back in Wisconsin. They had talked briefly, and then Chris tipped his head back, slumped down in the seat and was asleep before Paul had much of a chance to learn anything about him.

As he slept, Paul had the opportunity to look him over carefully. While he thought his clothing was odd (you don't see too many people out on the highway in green pajamas and slippers), he realized that this stranger was traveling with no luggage or bag of any kind. His demeanor, appearance and overall attitude assured Paul that Chris was neither a vagrant nor someone to be feared, but his attire and lack of belongings seemed mighty peculiar.

Paul promised himself that he would solve this mystery, but he considerately decided to do so through the course of conversation, rather than possibly embarrassing Chris by asking him directly. As Chris slept, Paul studied him carefully and began to sense that there was more than initially met the eye with this unusual stranger.

They had just passed the sign for Cedar Rapids, Iowa when the rising sun reflected off the side view mirror into Chris' eyes and awakened him.

Paul, keeping his curiosity at bay, had been driving for almost ten hours straight. He was pushing the legal limit and needed to find a truck stop to have a bite to eat, catch some sleep, get cleaned up and get back on the road again. He saw Chris open his eyes and stretch.

"I'm going to pull into the next truck stop to grab some breakfast and sleep," he announced to Chris.

Paul took the next exit onto the frontage road that paralleled the highway. He noticed a small farmhouse as they passed about a quarter mile before the entrance to the large open parking lot of the truck stop.

As Paul turned into the lot and pulled up next to one of the other forty or fifty eighteen wheelers, Chris said, "I'm going to take a little walk, but I'll be back before you're ready to go."

With that, Chris hopped down from the cab and headed back down the nearly deserted road toward the farmhouse.

The farmhouse was old and weathered. Although it was in need of a paint job, the porch was clean and tidy, nicely decorated with potted plants and flowers recently picked from the garden.

Momma and Poppa Horton had lived on the farm over 30 years. They had raised a son and two daughters, and somehow had managed to get by, despite the fact that the new larger and more efficient businessman farms had taken over most of the other smaller farms in the county.

They had been calling each other Momma and Poppa ever since Sonny, their oldest, had been a baby, and now everyone they knew did the same. In fact, most of the younger folks at church, their only social outing of the week, had never even heard them called by any other names.

Although farming had been a hard life, they loved each other with a deep "grown-together" love which had originally begun as physical attraction and teenage infatuation, but had grown to be an inseparable bond strengthened by years of working the farm together, raising a family, and which was based on a mutually shared faith in God and respect for each other.

The farm had left them little time for entertainment, but what had begun as a simple curiosity on Poppa's part had grown into a fascinating hobby for both of them. In the early years of their marriage, Poppa had bought Sonny a crystal radio kit as an educational toy. Poppa and Sonny built the radio together, but young Sonny lost interest almost immediately. Poppa on the other hand was intrigued. He sent away for more kits, then began to read and study about radio and television. Over the years his interest had spread to Momma. Their pride and joy was the HAM radio get-up that Poppa had built entirely by himself with the various component parts that he had ordered by mail from the Heathkit Company. He had done the wiring while Momma had read the instruction manual.

They enjoyed the HAM radio even more than the 21" TV which Poppa had also built from a kit. While most people were watching their favorite TV shows, Momma and

Poppa were studying their manuals or talking to strangers around the world.

When Chris approached the farmhouse that morning, Momma and Poppa were sitting at the kitchen table listening to the shortwave radio and having their second cup of coffee. Momma looked up and saw him walking up to the house.

"Well, will you look at this! Who do you suppose he is? Look Poppa, there's a stranger coming up to the house dressed in some kind of green pajamas."

Poppa turned, looked and sat back in his chair. Sure enough here was this nice-looking young man just about to reach their front porch. They watched, as without hesitation, he took three steps up in one jump and knocked on the screen door.

He could obviously see them through the hall into the kitchen, just as they could see him, but he politely knocked and waited for them to come to the door before addressing them.

"Momma, open the door for the young man. See what he wants. Maybe he would like some coffee."

Since the children had married and moved away, there hadn't been much new in their lives. They had given up trying to keep the farm up, basically subsisting on their social security check and what little savings they had managed to sock away over the years. Their only visitors, except for holidays, were those that came in by way of the shortwave. Generally, they were leery of strangers, but this one seemed different. Even from a distance, he had a friendly look about him that encouraged them to trust him.

"Good morning," Momma addressed Chris. "Would you like to come in?" As she opened the door, she felt a sense of confidence and security that she couldn't explain. Rather than being timid or reluctant to let this strange man into her home, she wanted him to come in. She hoped he would feel welcome and have coffee. While she was curious about why he was here, she had no fear or trepidation. She knew that this unusual encounter was for the good.

These thoughts surged through her mind more as a sensation than individual images. She was delighted that he was there with no apparent reason, yet she didn't question her feelings.

Chris walked in, followed Momma into the kitchen and accepted the coffee which was fresh-brewed, hot and tasty.

"It's a beautiful day for a walk," Poppa broke the silence. "Where have you come from?"

Chris smiled at them. "Thanks for the coffee, it really hit the spot. We've been driving all night and I really didn't sleep too soundly in the truck. I'm on my way out west and a truck driver was kind enough to pick me up in Wisconsin. I'm headed out to the desert to sort some things out, make some plans and organize my life and future, so to speak. Right now, I have a little problem that I hope you folks can see your way clear to help me with."

Momma and Poppa saw from his earnest expression that he wasn't the sort to beguile them. They wondered what his problem could be and how they could possibly help him.

From the quizzical look on their faces Chris saw that he should continue, "I find myself with no other clothes than these hospital greens, and I wonder if you might have some old clothes; perhaps some jeans, overalls and T-shirts that your son no longer wears."

"Our son?" Momma said, "How do you know our son?"

Chris glanced up at a framed picture of the two of them with their son, "I just guessed that maybe he had grown up and moved away."

Momma smiled. "You know, you're just about his size."

"He played quarterback on the high school football team," Poppa added proudly. "Was good enough for college, and even had some of the coaches from Iowa State come down and talk to him about a scholarship. He had his own ideas though. Got married right out of high school. Now he works in a factory making farm equipment over in Des Moines. Still married though; two little grandkids just as cute as a button. That boy and his wife, they're gonna make it. They're gonna be okay. So many of these kids get married too young, have kids and get divorced, but not Sonny, he's doing fine. I do wish that he'd gone on to college though, what with that scholarship and all . . . Listen to me, Momma, I'm just droning on. Son, if you need clothes, we've got plenty. Sonny left them here when he left and he'll never use them. They'll just rot in the drawer. Momma show --" he stopped. "What's your name again son?"

"Chris," he answered.

"Show Chris Sonny's clothes."

Momma led Chris to Sonny's old room and pointing out the dressers, welcomed him to anything he needed.

As Chris was trying on a pair of Levi's, he found a $20 bill in the pocket. After changing, he found Poppa and started to hand him the bill explaining his find. Poppa stopped him and said, "Son, maybe that $20 was meant for you. Frankly, it looks to me like you could use it. Just keep it and consider it our bet on you and your future."

Chris smiled and thanked him.

By the time Chris had left, they had filled an old duffel bag with as much as it would hold. Chris didn't volunteer as to why he found himself out in the middle of the country in need of clothes, and they never asked him. Frankly, they were happy to have the company and they were glad that they were able to help.

After Chris left, Poppa reached over to turn the shortwave back on, but the look on Momma's face stopped him.

"Momma, what is it?"

"Didn't you feel it? Didn't you feel something very unusual about that young man?"

"Well, he certainly was very nice, and I'm glad that we were able to help him, if that's what you mean."

"No Poppa, there was more, much more. The moment he came in the door, I knew there was something special about him. I can tell you one thing, call it woman's intuition or whatever you want, but we haven't seen the last of him; no sir, not by any means."

When Chris arrived back at the truck stop, Paul was snoring loudly in the sleeper. Chris went in to the trucker's lounge, took a shower, shaved, dressed in jeans and a white T-shirt, got a bite to eat and returned to the truck. Chris had dozed in the front while Paul slept.

Chris awakened as the truck lurched forward. Paul was back behind the wheel headed west. They drove in silence for awhile with Paul glancing over at Chris from time to time frowning.

44

Finally, he asked, "Where do you get those clothes?"

"Remember that farmhouse back by the truck stop?"

"Yeah."

"A nice couple that lives there gave them to me."

"You mean, they just gave you the clothes?" Paul was incredulous. "Why did they give them to you?"

"Because I needed them."

"But what did you tell them?"

"I told them that I needed clothes."

"But, didn't they ask why?"

"No. I guess it was obvious why."

Paul glanced at Chris again, shook his head and then drove on in silence.

Chapter 22

Eva had chosen nursing as a career while still in high school. The clean white uniforms and the antiseptic smell of doctors' offices and hospitals were like heaven to her in comparison to the farm.

After graduation from high school, she spent an almost unbearable summer helping out on the farm. She couldn't wait to go off to Madison where she had been accepted at the University of Wisconsin Nursing School.

When she finally entered college in September at age 18, Eva gave the appearance of a much older and sophisticated young lady than her years or background would have suggested. She was tall, shapely and carried herself with her long blonde hair falling gracefully down to the middle of her back. Her poise set her apart from the rest of the giddy freshman girls and although she certainly caught the attention of the entering freshman boys, she was clearly more interested in the upperclassmen.

She was still a virgin. Despite her, as she considered it, insatiable appetite for sex, and having lived under her parents' roof, she was afraid to experiment for fear it would get out of control. She often thought of herself like an alcoholic. She was worried that once she started having sex, she wouldn't be able to control it. Thus, like a recovering alcoholic, she had simply stayed away from men. Her only release had been her nocturnal self-indulgences during which time she had learned to fantasize and mentally experiment in every way imaginable.

Now that she was in college, she felt it was time to let herself go. Her years of hiding her passion and inner feelings, however, were not easy to shake off. She found that in class, and in her everyday interaction with students and professors, she was in no way different than she had been in high school.

Nighttime was different! She began to go to college mixers and fraternity parties with the hope of finding the right man for her first sexual encounter. Very quickly she learned that although there were a lot of guys at the mixers, they reminded her of the guys in high school.

Fraternity parties were certainly wilder, and there was no question that frequently following a night of drinking and wild dancing, many of the couples ended up in the sack together. For Eva though, neither the environment, nor the boys, were right for what she had in mind. A drunken "wham, bam, thank you ma'am" just wouldn't do. She wanted her first sexual experience to be not just memorable, but to be remarkable, unforgettable; the moon, the stars, fireworks with a never-ending grand finale.

After her disappointment at the available "men" in the fraternities, she began to frequent the many clubs in downtown Madison. She was underage, but no one ever carded her. Tentative at first, she soon learned that an air of confidence made for an easy entrance, and as a beautiful woman entering the bars alone, the bouncers never charged her a cover or minimum to get in.

On her fifth consecutive weekend of scouting clubs for the appropriate "first", she noticed a somewhat familiar young man sitting at the bar in Vahson's. It was a nice club with a dance floor and dining room where local groups would play soft rock to a young, but past college crowd.

He was dressed in blue jeans and a black turtleneck sweater, with a full head of soft, curly brown hair falling over his ears. She knew that she had seen this guy . . . but where?

He was maybe 25, nicely built with no sign of flab on his lean muscular frame. He was apparently lost in thought as he stared over his drink into the wall. He was absentmindedly twisting his cocktail napkin around and around. Completely oblivious to her inquisitive stare, she wondered how long he would sit there just gazing into space. "What could he be thinking of?" she thought.

Just then, he turned and looked directly at her. His dark brown eyes sparkled from across the room as he smiled, got up and approached her table.

"You recognize me, but you can't remember from where," he said, as if he had read her mind. "Would it help if I said, 'I think, therefore I am'?"

Eva laughed. Of course, this guy was the young professor who taught Introduction to Philosophy, one of the electives she had chosen. She had attended every class and had been fascinated by some of the ideas and concepts that they were reading about. She had found his lectures to be both enlightening and entertaining. Always late to class, since her Introduction to English Literature in the hour before was all the way over on the other side of campus, she had always found herself at the back of the huge lecture hall.

Now that she realized who he was, she couldn't believe that she didn't recognize him immediately, and was floored that he even knew that she was one of the 470 students attending this class.

"I'm sorry, I guess I was staring."

"That's perfectly okay. This is a rather different context than you're used to seeing me in, and since I was probably the last person you ever expected to see in here, it's no wonder that you couldn't put the name with the face."

"But how did you recognize me? We've never spoken and I'm always hidden in the back of the lecture hall."

"You'd be amazed at how much I can see from the podium. Especially when a girl as beautiful as you attends one of my lectures, I always notice. I'd like to introduce myself. You know me as Professor Palmer, your teacher in Introduction to Philosophy, but tonight I'd like you to meet Tim, a mixed-up guy who knows better, but would like to join you for a drink. Believe me, I could use the company. I don't know why you're here, especially alone, but I'm sure there's a reason. Maybe it would be good for both of us to have a drink . . . sit and talk."

Eva was somewhat taken back by his direct approach. He was neither awkward, nor did he show signs of an over-inflated ego. Being treated as an adult had an exhilarating effect on Eva. Her initial reaction was a slight flush in her face and neck which she hoped he wouldn't notice, that accompanied the overt sexual stirring within.

"What do you say? Can I buy you a drink? By the way, now that you know who I am, it's only fair that you tell me your name."

"Eva," she said. "My name is Eva. I'm here looking for, well, perhaps looking for you?" She couldn't believe the words as they came out of her mouth. "I'd love to have a drink . . . a seven and seven would be fine."

Tim sat down, waved to the waitress, and ordered her drink and Black Jack on the rocks for himself.

"Tell me about yourself," he said. "If you were looking for me, now that you've found me, let me know what makes you tick; who you are, where you're from . . . and what brings you tonight, here to this table, in this bar talking to me?"

His direct questions surprised, but didn't offend her. Here was a man who had experience. He was a philosopher and he clearly wasn't intimidated by her or afraid of rejection. Both his direct approach and his pointed questions might have seemed inappropriate to someone else, but they were welcomed by Eva.

She told him about her parents, the farm and high school. As she warmed up to the autobiographical soliloquy, she began to reveal her most secret desires and fears. She found herself telling him about her hatred of the farm, the reason she chose to go into nursing, the immaturity of the high school boys and her disappointment to find that little changed when she arrived at Madison. She told him how she worried that the longing within her would never be fulfilled. She opened up to him like she had never opened up to anyone ever before.

He listened intently, encouraging her without any sign of judgment. After about an hour, she looked across the table at him. She couldn't believe all the things that she had revealed. Somewhat surprised that she wasn't the least bit embarrassed by what she had said, she leaned across the table toward him and said, "I'm a real nut case, aren't I?"

"You think you're different, even abnormal. You think that you're all alone with your fears, your yearnings, your secret desires. You're afraid that your friends would reject you and your parents would be horrified. You have kept everything bottled up inside for years. Now you've surprised yourself by opening up so quickly to me. You're probably wondering right now, 'What must he think of me?'

"The fact is, Eva, there is no definition of normal. Just as some people's appetite for food is insatiable and they have a tendency to overeat, there are others who are by nature, lean and picky eaters. You described yourself

49

as a sexual alcoholic that abstains for fear of bingeing. You condemn yourself and believe that others would do the same for having a natural desire that you have no more control over than the color of your hair or your height. Further, you are basing your concern on things imagined and yet to be experienced. Maybe you're not as insatiable as you think.

"You were willing to tell me intimate details of your thought-life, because in essence I am a stranger who knows none of your family or acquaintances. Further, as a professor, you have confidence in me, and you became more comfortable with me when you realized that I was totally non-judgmental. You may also have been somewhat surprised that I don't consider your thoughts or desire to be beyond the range of normal."

Eva had never met anyone like Tim. He was so confident and straightforward. She felt at ease with him and the more he talked, the more she found herself attracted to him.

"Would you like another?" he asked.

She nodded in the affirmative.

Sipping her third drink, she looked directly in Tim's brown eyes and questioned, "You know just about everything about me. Other than the fact that you're a professor, I know just about nothing about you."

He smiled. "What would you like to know?"

"Everything! Where you're from, how you got here to Madison, and maybe most importantly, why you are here alone tonight."

"For the last three months, I have been staying home alone either reading or, once classes started, preparing lecture notes. I have buried myself in my work afraid to face a reality that will not go away.

"My wife and I were married in June, just after we graduated from college a few years ago. She was an art history major and I was a philosophy major. While I pondered man's unanswered questions, she saw a reflection of mankind in the world of art. Although our perspectives were very different, we fit together in every way like a hand in a kid-glove.

"We were married for four years. Early this summer, she had been asked to chaperon a group of high school students interested in art history on a tour of Italy.

It was to be a seven day trip with stops in Milan, Venice, Rome and most exciting for her, Florence. I had never seen her more enthusiastic about anything in her life.

"The tour left from Kennedy airport in New York at 7:00 p.m. on a Friday, so she had a mid-morning flight from Madison to New York. We had a nice breakfast before she left, although she kept looking at her watch for fear she would miss the plane. I drove her to the airport with plenty of time and kissed her at the curb. She insisted it would be silly for me to come in. 'Why waste the money parking only for a few minutes. It's so expensive.'

"Those were the last words that I heard her speak, and that was the last time that I ever saw her. When she arrived at Kennedy, she was riding the shuttle bus to the International Building when a limousine driver racing around the inner circle, late to pick up some VIP, had a flat tire on the left front side just as he was passing the shuttle on the right. The heavy limo careened to the left and smashed into the bus on a 45 degree angle hitting the precise spot where my wife was sitting.

"She never knew what happened. She was killed instantly."

Eva was distraught. There were tears in her eyes and she instinctively reached across the table to hold Tim's hand as the story unfolded.

"She had no family, other than me. I flew to New York, arranged for her cremation and flew her ashes back with me to Madison. Later I scattered them in the little garden outside the Philosophy Department office where she and I used to sit for hours, just talking. She loved that little garden."

Eva didn't want to hear any more. She didn't need to hear anymore. This poor man was alone and needed her to comfort him and be with him. Although she had originally been physically attracted to him, she now had almost forgotten the reason why she had come to Vahson's in the first place. Now she wanted to be with him, for him, not for her.

He sat there in silence obviously caught in memories of his wife.

He paid the bill without saying a word and they left. She followed his car back to his apartment which was actually a duplex about six miles away. He motioned for

51

her to park in front while he pulled into the garage. After parking, he came back out and led her through the garage to the small kitchen.

"Would you like a drink?"

"Yes, ah no." She thought better of another drink. She wanted to be totally clear-headed. After all, this was not only the event that she had been waiting for since puberty, but now, due to fate and circumstances, she found herself with an extraordinary man who was alone and in need of comfort at a time when she was available. No, she didn't want to spoil this opportunity with too much to drink. No way!

"I want to go to bed with you." There she had said it; simple and straightforward.

"Are you sure?"

In response, she reached up to him and placed her hands on either side of his face, ever so gently drawing him to her. She kissed him, just as a feather drops on a pillow, brushing her lips on his and then more firmly as the fingers of her right hand reached back and pushed up into the hair on the back of his neck. Her left arm extended down and encircled his waist.

He responded gently at first, but then pulled her to him with a strength and urgency that caught her off guard.

"It's been too long," he whispered, "too, too long!" He picked her up into his arms, and still kissing, he carried her into the bedroom.

This was it! She could hardly contain herself. When they reached the bed, they tore at each other's clothes, she helping him with her bra and he with his belt buckle. Things were now happening faster than she ever imagined.

Her long time fantasy was a tantalizing, almost unendurable foreplay followed by excruciatingly slow sex that would result in orgasm after orgasm. Reality was quite different. He had pushed her back down on the bed and was on top of her almost immediately. With no apparent concern for either her virginity or her psyche, he drove into her painfully and in less than thirty seconds, it was over.

Far from orgasm, she was in pain, shock and disbelief. What had happened to the sensitive philosopher;

52

the hurt widower who needed comforting. Where was the insightful, considerate human being that she so much wanted to share her first sexual experience with? Was this what sex was all about? How much worse than she had ever imagined. To add insult to injury, when he had finished, he rolled off of her, turned on his side facing away from her and was asleep almost immediately.

She just couldn't believe it. When she tried to snuggle up to him, he pulled away annoyed.

"It's late. I've got to get some sleep. Lots of work to do in the morning," he mumbled, and went immediately back to sleep.

Eva quietly rose, found her clothes, dressed in the dark and left. She had been hurt, insulted, but more than anything else, deeply disappointed. She now knew that she would never find satisfaction, that she wasn't normal, and that she would probably never achieve inner peace.

Weeks later, when she learned that Tim's whole story was a scam and that he preyed on innocent, unsuspecting college girls, she was angry but she really didn't care anymore. She had come to the conclusion that if she could be used, then so could men, and she had already learned that this could be very lucrative.

Now Eva didn't care if they were immature boys, drunken men, handsome or ugly. As long as they could pay the price, she didn't care. Oddly enough, some of the least likely, turned out to be the best lovers and frequently she found herself having multiple orgasms just as she had imagined. However, by this time, she had given up on the idea of being fulfilled or satisfied in an anymore meaningful way than physically.

In the same way that she had hidden her secret desires from her parents when she was a child, Eva was now the perfect nursing student by day and a highly paid call girl at night. Neither endeavor, although she was highly proficient at both, satisfied the inner hunger that never disappeared. Hunger for what, she wasn't exactly sure, but she now knew that sex wasn't it.

Chapter 23

Try as he might, Murray Greenbaum couldn't find the loophole. Tracking down the story, he summed it up in his notes. "John Doe discovered in Eden Prairie, Wisconsin. Recovered fully after three weeks in coma, doctors found no cause. Apparent total amnesia. Disappeared from the hospital. Reappeared at crime scene. Witnesses reported he touched a police officer, who had been gun shot at pointblank range, miraculously healing all wounds. John Doe again disappeared, current whereabouts unknown."

Murray didn't get it. The local agent, a man with years of experience and among the most highly rated, whom Murray knew and trusted completely, had reluctantly reported the facts in the case.

The agent knew that his report read like a supermarket tabloid, but as he said to Murray, "I've checked everything three times. The witnesses are all reliable and their stories are all consistent. They are all police officers, doctors, nurses or local reporters. The facts are the facts, strange as they may seem."

Murray was not a religious man, nor was he a believer in ESP or extraterrestrials or any of the other crazy explanations for this type of phenomenon. In this case, however, Murray had no plausible explanation for what happened with the mortally wounded police officer, other than some kind of miracle, and Murray didn't believe in miracles.

Murray was certain that there was more, much more than met the eye. He just couldn't figure out for the life of him what it was.

Chapter 24

For the second day in a row, a stranger approached their door as they sat in the kitchen drinking coffee. This time it was a man who had driven up in an expensive limousine, followed by several TV news trucks and cars filled with reporters.

They all crowded around the front porch as the well-dressed man from the limo knocked at the screen door.

"Better see what this is all about." said Poppa as he got up from the kitchen table. After a moment or two at the screen, he called over his shoulder, "Put on some more coffee, Momma, I think we ought to invite this fella in. He says we've just won $77 million dollars in the state lottery with that ticket I bought last week. Highest single winning ticket ever, he says."

Chapter 25

They were back on the highway. Paul had been silent for a long time and Chris seemed to be content just staring out the window watching the scenery go by.

Paul couldn't stand it any longer. "What's going on here? Who are you anyway?"

Paul had to confront Chris. He knew that this man was different and from their brief time together and what he had seen, he knew that Chris was something special. Paul had early-on decided to accept people for what they were without questions, because that was the way that he wanted people to accept him. For this reason he had, up until now, held back hoping that Chris would reveal who he was without his needing to ask; but it was too much, he just had to know.

Chris smiled. "Paul, we have a long ride ahead of us and I think I'm ready myself to accept who I am, so you might as well be the first person that I share it with.

"Have you ever seen pictures of the stars taken through a powerful telescope which show the reoccurring perfect geometric patterns and designs in the heavens? Or, have you ever studied the perfect balance of molecular structure or the symmetry of atomic particles? Have you considered the balance of nature; how the rain provides just enough water, the animals and natural fires give off the carbon dioxide needed by the green plant life, while plants generate the oxygen needed by animal life? Have you ever looked at a snowflake closely and noticed how perfect, yet unique, its crystal structure?

"Have you ever looked at the ebb and flow of the tides which create a seashore environment without which thousands of shoreline species could not exist; or the oceans themselves where the algae live in balance with the sea life, in the same way that the land plants and animals live in balance.

"All of this balance, harmony, organization and interaction is no cosmic accident. It is all part of a greater creation, something which man has tried to understand since time began. You must realize that man himself is part of this creation. However, as an intelligent being, man is not just a part of the created existence, he has an impact on it. While the rest of existence stayed within the bounds that the checks and balances of nature provide, man has evolved intellectually and has additionally become dependent upon and influenced by the balance of the society he has created.

"Man has moved beyond simple needs for the basic life-giving properties of nature such as oxygen in the air, availability of sunlight and abundant food which provided for early man as independent individuals. Today, individuals depend on, and take for granted, things which man has created, but are so technical, that only the specialists understand their own areas of expertise, and no one understands it all."

Paul was confused. "What do you mean?"

"This truck you're driving. Do you know how the engine works? Would you know how to design the molds which the steel is poured into to form the engine block with cylinders calibrated to thousandths of an inch? Do you know how your TV works or how signals are sent and received across the country, and around the world via satellites, cable, high-frequency and infrared waves?

"How does a jet plane fly? Why do fertilizers make crops grow better? What makes food preservatives work? How do you make a tin can. . . a drinking glass. . . a paper cup. . . a plastic bag?"

Paul wondered where in the world Chris was going with all of this, but he kept quiet, fascinated as Chris continued.

"Meanwhile, as technology has advanced providing untold luxuries and abundance, man has not grown emotionally. Greed, selfishness, jealousy and evil in all its many forms lurk just below the surface of society. Man today fights for territory, wealth and power just the same as the caveman did.

"Governments are fraught with corruption. Businesses seek only the almighty dollar. Individuals think only of themselves. History repeats itself with conquest after conquest. Be they military or economic. The old Machiavellian adage that 'power corrupts and absolute power corrupts absolutely', can be seen to be true in every level of society.

"The opportunity that technology has offered, to achieve a perfectly balanced world where man could live in comfort, peace and harmony, has been defeated by man's baser instincts. Man must change emotionally and spiritually to achieve the balance that will provide the world what mankind so desperately wants and is technologically capable of achieving.

"When nature goes out of balance, something occurs which pushes it back into balance. If, in the wilderness, the deer herd grows too large and endangers the vegetation, the wolf pack also grows until the deer population declines.

"The various species of plants and animals act as a check and balance with one another. Even the weather plays a role. Heat and drought are balanced by cold snaps and storms, with the end result providing exactly the right average temperature and the ideal average rainfall for the flora and fauna to not only survive, but to flourish, as the environmental variations create versatility and strength.

"Life is not desperately hanging on to existence. Life does not cower in the dark. In every instance, life thrives. It blossoms and grows exuberantly. It evolves and is self-improving, however, evolution represents a chronology of change within a creation so huge and magnificent that it is beyond man's comprehension. Man's theory of evolution only begins to identify the very tip of the iceberg.

"Man himself is part of that ebullient explosion of life, and man, the only thinking animal, has created more to improve life through technology than even society realizes. The problem is, it's just not working.

"You asked me who I am. I am simply the man who is here to correct the problem, to eliminate the flaw that prevents man from reaching his destiny. I am the intervention that occurs when things are out of balance in nature."

Paul pulled the truck over to the side of the road. He look straight at Chris, "Are you telling me that you are God? Are you sitting here in my truck telling me mankind is out of balance, and you're going to fix it?" Paul stared at Chris.

"Yes," said Chris, "I am." "Since there is no way for mankind to truly comprehend the totality of existence, and the harmony and balance within, the human concept of an omnipotent and omniscient God whose very being defies human understanding is appropriate, even though I didn't realize it myself in the beginning. I am not that God, but I was sent by him.

"At first, I didn't know who I was, or why I was here, but as time passed, I began to sense the need surrounding me. I could feel the pain and suffering. I realized that despite all the abundance, luxury and opportunities surrounding them, people were depressed and unhappy. I am a man sent to this world, for lack of a better term, because the world is not right, but can be."

Paul was stunned. Chris' news was incredible, yet Paul could not help but believe him. There was an infinite truth in this words, in his expression, and in his demeanor. "How are you going to change mankind . . . change the world?"

"I don't know yet," Chris said, "but, when I do know you can be sure that I'm going to ask you to help me."

"But Chris, you have no money, you have no car, you barely have any clothes. You have no home, no family, no place to go. How are you going to exist, much less change the world?"

Chris laughed. "Paul, when the flowers need water, what happens?"

"It rains."

"And do they have to hunt for nourishment?"

"No, it's in the soil."

"And how much effort do plants put forth to create the beauty of their flowers?"

Paul thought for a moment. "Well, I guess they just grow flowers as part of their nature. Just by existing, they bear flowers."

Chris looked at Paul, "And so it is with all of us. What happened when I needed a ride?"

"Well, I guess I came along."

"And what happened when I needed clothes?" Chris asked.

"Some farmer gave them to you."

"You see, Paul, worrying about surviving makes no sense. You don't have to worry about me, yourself or anyone else. Life is here and we, as part of that life, are here to flourish. Rather, we all need to make every effort to make the most out of the life that we have. When your time on earth is over, it's over. No amount of worry can

59

stop the inevitable."

"Chris, I just can't sit here and believe I'm riding along with some sort of human manifestation of a superior existence beyond human understanding. I've spent my whole life denying the existence of God. There was never any proof. Now I've seen you do some things that I can't explain, and I've certainly never heard anyone talk like you, and you don't seem to be crazy; but, and this is a big but, just because the snowflakes form in the shape of crystals and certain geometric patterns reoccur in space as well as in molecular structures, doesn't mean there is a God. I just don't believe God exists."

Paul wasn't really as sure of himself as he sounded, but years of cynicism, questioning and debating the subject made the question come out almost as a reflex, reflecting Paul's skeptical nature.

"Do you believe that you exist?" Chris asked.

"Of course I do," said Paul.

"Why?"

"Because I am here. I can think. I can talk. I'm here with you, so I must exist."

"OK," said Chris. "Do you believe your grandfather existed?"

"Of course."

"Why?"

"Because I remember him. He died when I was 19. I remember him very well."

"So even though he's not here, you're sure he existed?"

"Yes, very sure."

"And, what about your grandfather's great grandfather. You never saw him, nor heard him speak, or even met anyone who did; are you sure that he existed?"

Paul looked a little quizzical. "Of course he existed. If he didn't, I wouldn't be here. By definition, because I exist, so did he."

Chris nodded in agreement. "Paul, do you believe that the earth has existed forever?"

"No. Science has shown that the earth was once part of the sun." Paul was feeling a little uncomfortable with the direction of the conversation.

Chris realized that Paul saw where the conversation was leading. "Paul, we could keep going backward with

60

this exercise, but I think you get the point. The same logic which convinces you that your existence proves that your grandfather's great grandfather existed, also proves God's existence. Just as each new life is created and each new flower comes from a seed, the earth, moon and stars, and everything in the universe started with a creation; a creation that is proven simply by our very existence. We are here because life and its environs were created.

"Mankind is not able to comprehend the true concept of creation; where there was nothing, something appeared, but by our existence, we know that it happened. Unable to explain creation scientifically, man has defined creation through myths and religion. The Bible provides a wonderful accounting of many events that took place and tells many stores that are helpful in guiding man in his understanding of human behavior, but neither the Bible, nor any other book explains creation or the existence of God. Nor can I explain to you the creation, just as I can't explain my own existence. Man simply does not have the terminology or references to grasp these realities. However, I can assure you that I am here for the good of all mankind, and that together, with many others, you and I will cause the changes necessary to achieve harmony and balance that is so necessary for man's future."

"But, how?" was all that Paul could muster in response.

"Don't worry about that now. I need to be alone for awhile to figure everything out. That's why I'm going out west. I need to spend some time by myself, and I figure the desert is as good a place as any. When I'm ready, and need your help, you'll know."

Chapter 26

Murray was on the case. He was very excited. By chance, he happened to be reading one of the wire service reports on a $77 million dollar lottery winner in Iowa, and picked up on a seemingly meaningless comment made by the winner.

"'It's funny,' he had said, 'but we'd gone for two or three years without seeing a stranger out at the farm. Then, we have two strangers in two days. The first was a very unusual young man about our son's age, and build too, who showed up out of nowhere dressed in some kind of hospital pajamas. Said he needed some clothes, so Momma gave him some that Sonny had left behind. He was a nice fella, said he'd be back someday and that he would repay us for the clothes and our kindness. Then just the very next day, the man with the lottery shows up with all the TV cameras. Funny, two strangers in two days like that.'"

The quote went on about what Momma and Poppa planned to do with their new found wealth all of which was irrelevant to Murray. The fact was, like finding a needle in a haystack, he now had a lead on the John Doe from Eden Prairie; with the green pajamas, it had to be the same man.

Murray called in his two best agents, Tony Palmisano and Joe Aleo, two young men, both coincidentally from the same Italian district in Boston. He gave them the background on the John Doe. After he had finished and left them alone, Tony looked at Joe and said, "Madonne, the old man's finally cracked. Now he's got us chasing after disappearing miracle workers with amnesia."

Joe, a couple of years older, said, "Look, I've worked for Murray for five years. This guy has a real nose for what's important. If he says, 'find this guy,' then as far as I'm concerned it's serious business, and you and me, we're gonna do this right and by the book. I don't know who this botchagalup is, but we're gonna find him. Am I right, or what?"

Tony realized that Joe was right. Murray was famous for finding trends that no one else could see, solving the unsolvable. If Murray thought this was worthwhile, then he'd give it his best shot.

"Yeah, you're right. I guess we better get ourselves a ticket to Iowa."

After a thorough interview with the lucky lottery winner, they traced the John Doe's steps back to the truck stop where, after conversations with waitresses and the crew at the garage, they ascertained that the guy in the green pajamas had come in and had caught everybody's attention.

One of the waitresses with a good memory, stimulated by a $20 bill, remembered that his name was Chris, and that he was riding with a Muirfield Trucking driver named Paul. As she went on, the two agents could hardly believe their luck when she recalled that they were heading for Las Vegas with a load of meat. She had served both Paul and Chris, although separately, and as was her nature, she had tried to chit-chat with both of them.

It didn't take long for them to track back through the Muirfield dispatcher to learn that Paul had indeed gone on to Las Vegas and delivered his load. In fact, he had made two runs since then. The first back hauling a load of furniture from Harrah's in Las Vegas to Harrah's in Atlantic City. From there he had picked up a container of dinnerware at the Port of Newark, which he was on his way to deliver to Excelsior Industries, a housewares distributor in Pittsburgh, PA.

When the FBI agents finally caught up with him, Paul had just finished dropping off the container and was headed for the Sheraton in Warrendale, just south of Exit 3 off the Pennsylvania Turnpike. Sheraton was a step up from his normal Red Roof or Motel 6, but he'd been on the road for almost three weeks straight and Paul felt he owed himself a treat.

As he stepped down from the cab, he saw two men get out of the four-door, dark blue Olds 88, which had followed him into the parking lot. Paul could tell that they were cops of some sort by their vehicle, their clothes, and the way they were directly approaching him. They obviously were on official business. He wondered what in the world they could want with him.

"Is your name Paul Simons?" Tony asked without any introduction or small talk.

"Who wants to know?" Paul didn't like the officious and condescending attitude and for a moment thought he might play tough guy. After all, they hadn't identified themselves yet, and for all he knew, they could be hoods, not cops.

"FBI," Tony said as he and Joe flashed their badges.

Paul relaxed a bit. He knew he had done nothing wrong, and he knew if he cooperated, there would be no problem.

"Yeah, I'm Paul Simons. What can I do for you guys?"

"Why don't we all go inside and check in. I think we have a long night ahead of us. Maybe we could chat over dinner?"

Joe hoped that the friendly tone, and the invitation to dinner would help Paul to be at ease. Joe had realized immediately that their abrupt approach, good when apprehending criminals, only served to frighten law-abiding citizens. Their background check of Paul Simons showed him to be a loner, but there was no indication of any criminal activity. They needed to lighten up since all they wanted from him was information regarding his passenger of a couple weeks back.

"Dinner sounds fine with me. I don't mind if the FBI wants to buy me a steak, but what's this all about anyway?" Paul asked.

After they had checked in, they went to the hotel restaurant, ordered a drink and finally explained to Paul that they had information that he had picked up a young man outside of Eden Prairie, Wisconsin dressed in hospital greens. They wanted to know everything that Paul could tell them about this man; who he was . . . where he was coming from. Where he was going? Why was he traveling west? Where had Paul left him off? Anything at all that he could remember . . . no detail was too small.

"Well, what can you tell us?" asked Joe.

Chapter 25

The bright lights of Las Vegas dazzled Chris as he stood in front of Harrah's casino. It was 8:00 p.m., Paul had finished loading his new cargo of furniture and had headed for the east coast about two hours earlier. Chris had wandered up and down the strip absorbing the sights and sounds, as he watched the people.

There were conventioneers spending a few days in Vegas on business, but with the primary intent of having as good a time as company expense accounts would allow. There were the down-and-out losers. Some, he imagined, had come to Las Vegas to make their fortune, and ended up doing the opposite. Now they were homeless men and women living in the back alleys and begging, as they dodged the ever vigilant police.

There were the girls. Everywhere he looked he saw beautiful young women. They had come to Las Vegas to be showgirls . . . some made it, some didn't. They became waitresses, cashiers, dealers, sales girls or in many cases, full or part-time prostitutes. Although prostitution was not legal in Las Vegas itself, other counties had legalized it and Las Vegas authorities looked the other way, as long as it was discreet.

There were little old ladies and widows, gambling with their husband's insurance money. There were the high rollers whose rooms, meals, shows and drinks were all "comped", and were expected to bet heavily every day, which they did. There were the honeymooners from all over the U.S.A. Young kids who probably would never have the opportunity to see this type of glitz, glitter and excitement ever again, and were willing to throw away thousands of hard-earned dollars for the experience.

Chris shook his head in dismay as he watched this parade of humanity stream by. Las Vegas was the epitome of greed and avarice. It offered a false promise of prosperity, a fool's paradise.

Chris needed to think, to plan. This clearly was not the place to do it. He decided to head out into the desert first thing in the morning.

When he entered the casino, Chris didn't have so much as a dime in his pockets. He wore a pair of Sonny's old Levis and a white T-shirt. He drew no attention as he entered since the crowd ranged from sequins and tuxedos to cutoffs and sandals. He just blended in as part of the crowd, completely unnoticed by security, or anyone else, as he entered the main gambling hall.

After looking around for a minute, Chris sat down at an empty seat at a roulette wheel between a tall middle-aged woman on his left, and a noisy, somewhat obnoxious man in a light blue business suit and white Stetson hat on his right. When he failed to make a bet after several spins of the wheel, the dealer explained to him that he would have to start betting or relinquish his seat, "house rules."

"I have no money," Chris said in a matter-of-fact tone.

"Well, I'm afraid that you can't sit at the table then," replied the dealer as he glanced over his shoulder at the pit boss who began to walk over.

Just then, the conventioneer in the blue suit and cowboy hat said, "Hard on your luck, eh? Here, take this $10 chip. I don't like to see them push anybody around. Go ahead, take it!"

"Thank you," Chris said. He took the chip and placed it on number 3.

"Wait a minute," the man in the blue said. Don't you want to spread it around a little bit? At least bet on red or black, odd or even. Give yourself a fifty-fifty chance." He was obviously a bit annoyed that this bozo was going to lose his ten bucks with one spin of the wheel.

"No," said Chris, "I think I'll leave it on 3."

"All bets down," said the croupier as he spun the wheel and dropped the chrome-plated steel ball. The ball bounced around for awhile and then landed solidly on 3.

"Well, I'll be damned!" said the man in the blue. "Son, you've just won yourself $350."

After his payoff, Chris returned $10 back to his benefactor and placed the $340 balance on the 3 again. The croupier called the pit boss over for approval, and after receiving the nod, spun the wheel. Everyone's eyes at the table were glued to the ball, and a gasp rose in unison followed by applause and cheering as the ball once again settled squarely on the 3.

In two spins of the wheel, Chris had turned $10 into $11,900. A crowd had gathered as the pit boss came around to supervise the payoff, and to carefully observe what might happen next. From experience, he knew that there were infrequent incredible runs of luck, and he wanted to be sure that he did everything possible not to let it happen on his shift.

When Chris indicated that he wanted to let the entire $11,900 ride for the third time in a row on the three, the crowd went crazy. Failing to dissuade Chris from this madness, the pit boss told the dealer to shut down play at that table until he could find the floor manager. By this time, word had spread throughout the casino and security had to cordon off the table while Chris and his fellow players waited for play to restart.

During a brief discussion with the casino manager, the floor manager had figured the odds of hitting the same number three times in a row at 2.14 out of a million. They told the pit boss to allow the play.

Several hundred people were crowded around the cordoned-off table when the dealer spun the roulette wheel. Sweat was beading on the pit boss' forehead, and tension was so high the room felt electric. Chris calmly watched the little silver ball with an anticipatory smile on his face and showed no emotional change what-so-ever when it landed on the 3 and held.

The pit boss was stunned. The dealer was in shock. He had never seen anything like this before. This guy walks in calm as a cucumber with no money. Some loudmouth hands him $10 and for no apparent reason, with three spins of the wheel, he walks away with $416,500. Unbelievable!

"No way!" yelled the floor manager as he watched through the ceiling peep. "Nobody's that lucky. Nobody."

Before agreeing to the bet, he had made sure that the video cameras were set up so that the play could be viewed later from every angle, if need be. While Chris was instructing the pit boss to place the money in an account in his name at the hotel, the floor manager and casino manager were reviewing the tapes.

"This guy was just incredibly lucky. We've watched the tape five times and nothing. Nothing is unusual," said the floor manager.

"Let's slow it down -- see if we can pick up anything in slow motion." suggested the casino manager.

They watched as Chris placed the bet. He placed eleven one thousand dollar chips and nine one hundred dollar chips on the number 3. He was sitting on one of the plush stools right in the middle of the table. Both of his hands were visible and on close inspection, he wasn't even touching the table with any part of his body. They watched in slow motion as the dealer spun the wheel and released the ball. Round and round it went, until it stopped naturally on the 3.

"What was that?" asked the casino manager.

"What was what?"

"What was the quick flash of light around the ball just before it dropped?"

The floor manager reran the tape. This time he saw it too. What they both had originally thought that they had seen as a quick reflection of casino lights when the tape was running at normal speed, now appeared as a very brief, but readily identifiable aura of color that surrounded the shiny steel ball for about an eighth of a second before it stopped on the 3.

"What the Hell was that?" repeated the casino manager. "Bring that guy in. I want to check him for electrical devices." While they waited, they ran the tapes over and over again.

Chris had not been out of the pit boss' sight for one second since the win. In fact, he had not moved from the stool and was talking congenially with the dealer and security people, waiting for them to bring a receipt for his winnings.

When the pit boss told him that the manager wanted to see him, Chris complied without a question or complaint, and followed the pit boss, with two security guards at his side, toward the elevator.

They were all business when Chris entered the plush manager's office. They watched him carefully as they replayed the tape, first at regular speed, and then again in slow-mo. Chris' expression didn't change in the slightest as he watched. There was no sign of concern, fear, intimidation or guilt. Even when the momentary burst of inexplicable color surrounded the ball, Chris didn't flinch or even indicate that he had seen anything unusual.

After the tape was finished, there was a long

silence, each side apparently waiting for the other to speak.

"How did you do it?" The floor manager smiled for the first time. "We've checked the ball and the wheel. They're perfectly normal. You haven't been out of our sight since the third hit and you have no concealed device of any kind, yet you were clearly controlling the ball. How did you do it?"

Chris learned forward in this chair. "It is unusual for the ball to land on the same number three times in a row, isn't it? I assure you gentlemen, I didn't control the ball. I think that your pit boss told me that the odds of the ball hitting the same number the third time were about 2 in a million. If, indeed that is correct, then I will agree that something is controlling the ball, even if it is only the odds. How many people have played at that table before me? Sooner or later, the three was bound to come up three times in a row. It just coincidentally happened when I was betting. Perhaps it was simply fate that caused me to sit down at that particular table at that particular time. Maybe, because I need the money, it came to me. Sometimes things happen that way.

"Inexplicable things often happen, that later seem to have happened for a reason. A person hesitates to check his watch before crossing a street, only to discover, had he not hesitated, a speeding auto coming from nowhere would have hit him. Another person misses his plane due to an unexpected traffic jam where there's never been a traffic jam before, later to find out that the plane had crashed with no survivors. Everyone has experienced this sort of uncanny situation and now, I've hit the number 3 three times in a row. I agree, it appears that something is in control, but I can assure you again, it's not me."

They looked at Chris with skepticism and disbelief. "How do you explain the instant burst of color that surrounded the ball just before it hit the number?"

Chris grinned, "I can't. It's your ball and your roulette wheel, you tell me. Now, if you haven't anything further, I would like to find a room, take a bath and get some sleep."

Confounded by their lack of evidence and Chris' comments, but not wanting to let him go, they offered him a "comp" room and meals as long as he wanted to stay.

"We will want to talk about this further. In the meantime, we hope you enjoy the hotel, shows and restaurants, but we must ask you to stay out of the casino until this matter has been fully investigated."

"What about the money?" Chris asked with a twinkle in his eye.

"Oh, the money is yours. You won it and it's yours to spend wherever and however you want . . . unless, of course, we can prove that you won it by cheating." The floor manager smiled. "Then, you will have to pay it back and we will have you arrested for stealing."

In actual fact, in cases such as this, the hotel probably wouldn't press charges, not wanting the bad publicity, but the floor manager wanted to see what kind of reaction Chris would show.

"Great," said Chris. "I'm going to go down and check in. Would you be so kind as to call down to the front desk to arrange for my room?"

The floor manager nodded to the pit boss who picked up the phone. The security guards opened the door and Chris left the office looking forward to a good night's sleep.

The next morning when the hotel manager called his room, he found that Chris had already checked out. The next call was to the head cashier and the manager was relieved to learn that all of the money was intact in Chris' account except for $2,000 which Chris had withdrawn in cash that morning.

"Oh well, I guess he doesn't like the accommodations," he muttered to himself. "But he'll be back for the money! By then, maybe we'll have figured this out."

Chapter 28

Chris was rolling west. He had rented a large R.V., and was headed for a little town in the Nevada desert called Beaches Flat. The R.V. dealer had said there was a quiet R.V. park where someone could be alone without fear of being disturbed.

Chris had paid cash in advance, which covered the vehicle and insurance, and left him with about $500 cash in his pocket. He wasn't sure how long he was going to be in the desert, but he was certain that he had plenty of money; if not, he could always drive back to Harrah's and withdraw more money from his account. Money was, however, the furthest thing from his mind.

As he had watched the slow motion tape of the steel ball landing on the 3, he was deeply moved by the quick flash of the colors, which instantly brought back to him the memory of the serenity of his origin.

He realized the symbolism of this event. He had needed the money, and the power from whence he came had sent it to him. Just as when Paul had needed the compressor to be fixed, the colors had appeared and the repair miraculously made. Now, mankind was in need of fixing and he had been sent as the repairman.

Chris had sensed this from the beginning, but now it was very clear to him. He was here on earth to make the difference, to put mankind on track, to "land humanity on the winning number." A seemingly impossible task, but to Chris, whose destiny it was, there were no doubts. He knew he would be successful, just as he had known that the ball would land on the 3, even though he hadn't actually made it happen himself. He knew it would be done, because he believed it could be done.

Driving down the highway toward the desolate crossroads in the desert known as Beaches Flat, the beginning of a plan was already formulating in this mind.

The road was straight as an arrow and stretched out in front of Chris as far as the eye could see, until it tapered down into a thin line and then disappeared into the horizon. Looking in the rearview mirror, Chris noted that behind him was a duplication of the view in front; a thin line of asphalt vanishing in the distance. He guessed that he could see ten to fifteen miles in each direction, and marveled at the fact that in all the distance, there was no sign of civilization. The desert was all around him and he felt a sense of solitude and tranquility engulfing him as he drove down the highway.

At first it appeared as a dark speck on the horizon, but as he drove further, he realized the speck was a dark blue sports car pulled over, or perhaps broken down on the side of the road. While he was still perhaps a mile away, Chris saw the driver's side door open and a man step out. The man moved into the middle of the road and began waving his arms. The closer Chris came, the more frantic the waving.

Chris slowed the R.V. as he neared the stopped automobile. The man was obviously signaling him to stop. The sports car was a dark metallic blue late model Corvette and the man fit the look of the car. He was young, perhaps 25, with black hair slicked straight back. He wore a large gold medallion around his neck. As he pulled up, Chris also noticed an expensive Rolex watch and shiny new Italian loafers.

"What's the problem?" Chris asked climbing out of the R.V., as the sharply dressed young man now approached him.

"Goddamned Vette! I just bought it. Only driven 150 miles or so, and the Goddamned thing conks out. Anybody with you in that R.V.?"

"No, I'm traveling alone and I'm afraid I don't know much about Corvettes, but you're welcome to come with me until we reach a service station or a telephone."

Chris was warm and friendly despite the fact that he sensed an element of danger in this encounter.

"No, that won't be necessary. I'm not the one that needs the ride." The flashy young man reached into the open door of the Corvette and pulled out a snub-nosed .38 Special from under the driver's seat. "I think that you'll be the one stuck out here in the middle of nowhere. Gimme your keys!"

Chris reacted calmly. "Look, I'd be happy to take you anywhere you want. I'll even go back to Las Vegas. I stopped to help and I still would be pleased to help you. There's no need for violence."

"So you want to help. OK, let me see your wallet.

72

Take it out of your pocket slowly, no fast moves and throw it over to me."

While Chris obeyed the instructions, the young man kept the gun aimed right at Chris' chest.

"Almost $500, not too bad. You got any more money, maybe back in the R.V. somewhere?"

"No, that's all the money I have. If you need it, take it, it's yours. I hope that you will find it helpful."

"Don't be a smartass. Any more wise remarks and you're a dead man. Now, lie down on the ground and don't even think about getting up until the R.V. is out of sight."

Chris lay there for a minute or two. He looked up and could see the R.V. as it diminished in size in the distance headed back toward Las Vegas. Chris stood up and started walking.

"Well, I wanted to be alone in the desert," he mused. "I couldn't be more alone than this."

After he had walked two or three minutes, he noticed that two cars were rapidly approaching. He thought of flagging them down, but decided that his destiny had led him out here to this barren strip of desert, and that he would just walk for awhile.

Chris was almost on top of it before he saw the dirt road that headed north off the main highway. Actually, it was more of a jeep track. For no particular reason he could pinpoint, Chris turned up the track. He felt that he was being guided toward some unknown destination, but he didn't know why, or to where. He really didn't care where, he just needed a place to think and to plan, and to really let the truth settle in as to who he was.

Chris had walked approximately six miles following the jeep trail. The desert wasn't quite so flat anymore and he had long since lost sight of the main highway in the rise and fall of the boulder-strewn hills. The only signs of life were the cacti and an occasional sound that must have come from a snake, desert rat or some other desert varmint which scurried or slithered away as he approached.

Much to his surprise, Chris finally came upon a little shack that had been built out of old shipping crates. There was no sign of life, but he immediately saw why the shack had been located in that particular spot. Someone, at some point in time, had discovered that there was water below this location and had dug a well.

Very thirsty from the long walk, Chris hoped that although it obviously hadn't been used for awhile, there would still be water in the well. He began to pump the handle up and down. Slowly and carefully at first, but when there was no result, he began to pump faster and faster, but to no avail. He suddenly realized that even if there was water below, the pump had long since dried out and would have to be primed before it would work. He smiled at the irony.

The shack had windows on each side and a simple wooden door hung on three hinges. There was a padlock on the latch, but it had been left unlocked. Chris stuck his head in the door.

Looking around he saw evidence that someone had actually lived in the shack, but had obviously abandoned the place long ago. There was an old blue and white striped tick mattress on the primitive wood floor. Several orange crates had been used as tables, bookshelves and for storage, and there was an old oil lamp for light. At first, he thought it was empty, but on closer inspection, Chris realized that the dusty one liter bottle of Polar Water that lay in the corner was not only full, but sealed as well.

Chris' thirst came back to him with a passion. The sight of water made him realize how parched he was and how badly he needed a drink. He picked up the bottle, wiped it off on his sleeve, twisted the cap, raised it to his lips . . . and stopped.

The thoughts came quickly, "This bottle will quench my thirst and get me back to the highway comfortably, but if I use it to prime the pump, then I can stay here until I have time to sort things out."

He was excited. This was the place. Yes, this was the place where he could think without distractions.

He felt a glow of affirmation as he took the bottle outside and primed the pump. It never even occurred to him that the pump wouldn't work after it was primed, or worse that there might no longer be water below.

The water came gurgling up from the well. Chris laughed, washed his face and then put his whole head under the spout. "Yes, this is the place!" he thought.

After washing, he went back in the shack, lay down on the mattress and as he drifted off into a deep, deep sleep, the colors began to emerge once again. Chris could feel himself drawn into the undulating waves of multi-colored light. He became the center and focal point of the radiating 360 degree rainbow and was one with its existence. This time he knew that when he awoke, he would remember everything. He would be prepared for the next step in his incredible journey.

The waves of color rolled over, in and around Chris as the reality of his hot ramshackle surroundings faded. His very being had become a part of the infinite symphony of color. He was still conscious of everything that had transpired since awakening in the hospital and all the memories, impressions, emotions, sensations, hopes, beliefs, faiths, as well as the turmoil, insecurities, ill-will, dismay, discouragement, jealousies, sadness and all of the other intangible feelings and sensations that he had absorbed from those around him.

The pulsations had slowed down into a steady rhythmic pulse and with each wave he experienced total recall of a stage in the history of the world beginning with the origin. He suddenly realized that the rainbow of undulating colors was simply the way that his human nerves and brain were able to picture the unimaginable beauty of the everlasting. The colors had always been, and would always be.

Chris also realized that the concept of time was also a human invention to relate to the passage from one image-state to the next; he likened mankind to a blind man sitting in a dark room with the light off. When suddenly the light is turned on, the blind man may sense the warmth of the bulb and may be pleased by the comfort of the warmth, but meanwhile cannot recognize the primary effect of the light, for he does not have the visual sense to fully appreciate it.

Beyond the ever-present origin, Chris saw the creation of the sun, the stars and the surrounding universe. With another wave of prismatic beauty, he saw the birth of living creatures and watched the evolution from the first living cell to the existence of man. For Chris, an instant was the same as forever in the world of colors. He watched as the predawn flora and fauna flowed and evolved into the age of dinosaurs. He viewed the emergence of man and smiled inwardly as he realized that the span of man's existence on earth compared to the dinosaur's longevity as an inch compares to a yardstick.

In an eternal moment, Chris watched the intellectual development of man and noted the curious leapfrogging effect caused by the miraculous injection of concepts and ideas which had resulted in the accelerated geometric progression of man's achievements. The sparks of genius that came to a few cavemen in diverse parts of the world, enabled them to harness fire, create the wheel and develop tools. The recognition of gravity, the theory of relativity; these were examples of certain individuals making great intellectual leaps, far beyond the capabilities of their peers, with no apparent reason other than it was "time" for those discoveries to take place.

The thinkers, inventors and philosophers such as Sir Isaac Newton, Albert Einstein, Plato, etc. were simply the instruments by which this "needed" information had been introduced to man.

Chris saw the formation of primitive religions as man looked to quell the fear of the darkness, the unknown, and insolvable. He watched religion grow in its various forms and saw how frequently the structure became more important than the message; the form more important that the content.

He watched the development of society from the first formation of primitive bands of wanderers to the development of great civilization with complex laws and politics. Chris mused as he realized that regardless of how diverse the sociopolitical path, every social system in existence since the beginning of man had ultimately failed. Sadly, in most cases all of the elements for success had been there. Whether it was the mores and ethics espoused in the Old Testament, the new covenant between the individual and God as offered by Christ in the New Testament, the simple Buddhist belief that every action taken today will have an impact on tomorrow, and that all life is a series of connected interacting cycles; in every religion, in every society, the concept of doing right by your fellow man was the fundamental belief. Nevertheless, in every case, society had ultimately fallen due to greed, avarice, the corruption of power and the baser evil instincts of man.

While man had been tracking at breakneck speed intellectually with one technical breakthrough after

76

another, the human or emotional side had not only not been evolving at the same rate, it had apparently ceased to evolve. The intellectual injections of genius which had stimulated man's progress scientifically had not been matched from the spiritual, emotional or human side at all.

In short, the men riding the rockets to the moon, orbiting the earth, splitting the atom, creating miracle drugs, etc., had the same base instincts, the same emotions and the same unanswered spiritual questions as did the caveman.

Suddenly Chris knew exactly why he was here, what he was to do, and how he was to do it!

His semi-dream state had kept him in the shack for almost two weeks with nothing to eat, and only water to drink. Now that he knew what he had to do, he needed to get out of there and find a phone. He had to call Eva, Paul Simons and the old couple in Iowa that had given him clothes, and there were many others just like them, all over the world that he would be contacting.

The excitement rose in Chris to a fever pitch. His vision of the future was now clear to him and he couldn't wait to get out of the desert and get started. It was only later, much later, that he even thought of stopping to eat.

Chapter 29

"Look, I dropped my load of meat at Harrahs in Vegas and I dropped the guy you're looking for off at the same time. That's all I know."

Of course, that wasn't all that Paul knew. He knew that Chris was the most extraordinary man that he had ever met. He knew that Chris was going to call upon him at some time in the future and that he would drop everything to be with him, and help him with his mission.

He had no idea what the FBI agents wanted Chris for, but he couldn't imagine that it would be helpful to Chris to have them on his back. The fact was that he really didn't know where Chris was planning to go after Vegas. So, he wasn't really lying to them. He just wasn't going to volunteer any information.

"By the way, why are you looking for him? Has he committed some sort of crime? Is he dangerous? Seemed like a pretty nice guy to me," Paul offered.

"FBI business," Palmisano said. "We aren't allowed to discuss the nature of our investigation at this point. Here's my card. If you think of anything else, or remember anything . . . anything at all which might help us find him, please give us a call."

Having finished their dinners, the two agents excused themselves and left Paul alone at the table. Joe winked at Tony and said, "Las Vegas, here we come."

Chapter 30

Poppa hung up the phone. He was smiling.

"Momma, remember that nice young man who stopped by the day before we won the lottery? He just called. It seems he needs our help again. Let me get you a cup of coffee and we can sit out on the porch while I explain this to you. Momma, I don't know how to say this, but I've never felt so alive in all my life . . . wait until you hear this!"

Chapter 31

It was 7:00 a.m. when the phone rang. Eva was at the dressing table brushing her hair. As soon as she heard his voice, she knew who it was and just the sound brought back a flood of memories. For an instant, she was back in the hospital, back in his arms. There was no rationale for the sense of safety and peace that she felt, or the warmth or inner glow that his simple 'Hello, Eva?' had caused, but there it was.

As she listened to him talk, she closed her eyes and as his words engulfed her, she felt as if the mental burdens that she had carried for so many years were being lifted as if by magic, and that she had risen above her everyday problems as if floating on a rainbow.

It had only been a few days earlier that she had found out for sure that she was pregnant, and she knew it was his. She had told no one as yet, and although for the briefest of moments she considered telling him as he talked about the future, she began to realize that the impact of this extraordinary man was going to go far beyond her life, her baby, and those around her, so for now anyway, she would keep quiet.

Eva was incredulous that she of all people had been chosen, not only to play a meaningful role in the events that were about to happen, but to carry his baby as well. For awhile, the baby would be her secret. He had too many other important things to worry about. There would be plenty of time to tell him later.

Up until now, the only ray of light in Eva's life had been her encounter with Chris as the John Doe in the hospital. After he had disappeared, her heart wouldn't agree, but her intellect told her to forget him; that she would never see or hear from him again. Now, here he was and the bond between them was instantaneous and forever.

After she hung up, she sat for a few minutes savoring the moment. The longer he had talked, the happier she had become. So intent was she on the message, that it didn't even occur to her that it was unusual for a life to be totally changed by one phone call. Hers was, and she loved it. Her life, her outlook and her entire being now made sense. Best of all, she knew who she was and where she was headed. She felt a glow coming from her inner being. Finally, she knew what it was that she had been yearning for all of these years. As for the baby, what the future held in store, she couldn't possibly imagine, but ecstatic optimism would be an understatement if one were trying to describe Eva's feelings.

She looked forward to Chris' next call. Meanwhile, there was a great deal of work to do and the first step was to call Momma and Poppa, and then get to the library. She had some studying to do!

Chapter 32

Between her nursing job and her nocturnal activities, Eva had managed to accumulate quite a little nest egg which she thought might be useful in helping Chris, but after she realized the magnitude of the undertaking that Chris had proposed, she recognized that her savings were a mere pittance. Nevertheless, Chris had seen her willingness to give it all. More importantly, she herself now realized that suddenly she was free, and had been willing to give up everything, just because he had asked.

She marveled at the idea that a brief encounter, during which he had not even spoken, followed by a simple telephone call, had changed her life. In her mind, it was as simple as the flip of a switch. When the light came on, it was immediate, full and complete. Where there had been darkness and doubt, there was now light and faith.

Eva had known that night in the hospital, but she had been unable to put into thoughts or words what she knew. Even now that he had spoken to her and called upon her for help, she still couldn't put her emotions, faith and devotion into truly intelligent thoughts, or she would have told him how she felt. Because of him, she was now free from her life long inner torment, and she knew that Chris was with her, even if he was 2,000 miles away.

Chapter 33

Agents Palmisano and Aleo arrived in Vegas late on a Tuesday night. Like everyone else who arrives in Las Vegas, they couldn't resist doing a little gambling before going to bed. After all, they rationalized, "it's too late to work, and we are here!"

The next morning they began the painstakingly careful process of tracking down Chris. Much to their surprise and delight, they hit pay dirt on the second visit. They had shown the FBI artist's sketch of Chris to the security guards at Harrahs and two of them immediately recognized him, and remembered that he called himself Chris, although they couldn't remember his last name.

"No problem, though," said one of them. "He still has money in an account with the cashier. A lot of money. this guy won a bundle in a very short period of time . . . almost half a million dollars in three spins of the roulette wheel."

Agents Palmisano and Aleo looked at each other. "How is that possible?" asked Joe.

"I don't know, but I think that he hit the same number three times in a row betting all of his winnings each time. How he did it, nobody knows, but the guys in the front office are pretty upset about it."

"What do you mean?"

"Well, they didn't believe that it was legit. I mean, the odds are something like two in a million. Anyway, there was something funny, a light or something, that hit the ball just before it stopped. They caught it on video tape. Later they tore the table apart; pulled up the carpet and floor boards below the table; even cut the steel ball into pieces. When they found nothing, they closed down the entire area and scanned for electronic devices, and still came up with zip.

"Naturally they had searched the customer for anything unusual on him, but as you probably had guessed, they found nothing. This has never happened around here before. We've had big winners and we've caught cheaters, but nothing like this. They're sure this guy cheated . . . they just can't figure out how."

Palmisano and Aleo spent the next three days at

Harrahs. They interviewed gamblers, guests and staff. They watched the videos over and over at normal speed, and in slow motion. Despite their very professional questioning and observations, they essentially learned nothing more than the overview provided by the security guard.

When they called in their report to Murray, he advised them to stay at Harrahs, using the casino/hotel as their headquarters while they branched out to find Chris. One thing Murray was sure of, Chris would be back in contact with the cashier to collect the balance of the money.

During the first three days of the investigation, the two agents had called every airline, auto rental and travel agency in Las Vegas, but had come up with no leads. On the fourth day, on a hunch after watching so many R.V.'s drive down the strip, Joe called the largest R.V. dealer in town.

"Yes, we did rent a very nice R.V., not a large one, but a very nice used R.V. to a Chris Lambert. He paid in advance with cash. He said something about spending some time alone. No, I'm afraid he didn't provide us with a specific destination.

"His license? Well yes, that was a bit unusual. He had a brand new temporary license from the state of Nevada and he gave Harrahs as his address. When we called over there, they confirmed that he had been a guest, had apparently checked out temporarily, but they expected him back as he had left a relatively large sum of money in his account with the cashier.

"You learn not to ask a lot of questions out here, and in case you're wondering, it's not unusual for people to pay with cash.

"Sure, I can give you the license number and description of the vehicle."

As Joe took down the information, he thought to himself, "Chris, we've got you now!"

Chapter 34

Agents Palmisano and Aleo were ecstatic when they learned that the local police had picked up the R.V., and had Chris in custody. Although he was refusing to cooperate and insisting that he was not Chris, they were sure they had him.

"Who the hell is that?" Joe Aleo looked at the local police sergeant. "That's not the guy we're looking for."

"Well, he's the guy who was driving the R.V. which you had an APB out on."

"Hey slick," said the sergeant, "tell the nice man from the FBI who you are."

"I'm Tino Salvucci. Look, all I know is this guy paid me $500 bucks to return this R.V. to the dealer in Vegas. I don't know nuthin' else, and I'm not sayin' nuthin' else 'til my lawyer gets here."

Within two hours Tino was free. His lawyer pointed out that there had been no crime committed, no complaint and that there was nothing to hold him for.

Agents Aleo and Palmisano had no choice but to let Tino go. After all, the R.V. wasn't stolen and there was no way to refute Tino's story. Their years of experience and gut instinct told them that his story didn't ring true, but the law was the law and they couldn't hold him.

Tino took the next plane to New York. He figured he better take a powder. Nothing had gone right lately, he thought.

"First the stolen Vette breaks down in the middle of the desert. Then, I have the unbelievable bad luck to steal an R.V. from some guy who's wanted by the FBI. Time to lay low for awhile." These thoughts drifted through his mind as he drifted off to sleep on the 747 headed for New York.

Chapter 35

Momma and Poppa had never been so sure of anything in their lives. Chris' phone call had given them new reason to live. It had provided them with the opportunity to participate in the event of a lifetime; no, the event of the millennium. They had been called to participate in what they had come to think of as the final covenant. This was no religious nut or lunatic with a pipe dream. Chris was the real thing. Even though they didn't exactly understand, at this point, how their role would fit into the total scheme of things, they were convinced by what Chris had said, that it was vital.

They were delighted that they had been called upon at this late stage in their lives. They believed that this was the reason that they were alive. All the hardships on the farm; the years of solitude after the children had left; the lean years when they had found their only solace in each other and the Bible; all these life experiences had been preparing them for this challenge. They just hadn't known it.

Although they had been faithful to their religion, they had certainly not thought of themselves as Saints. Rather, they considered themselves to be dirt-poor farmers, who like many of their neighbors, put their trust in God to carry them through the tough times.

First the stranger, then the lottery and finally the call! They felt 20 years younger and began to attack the project which Chris had laid out for them with a vigor that they hadn't experienced since they were first married. There was so much to do and so many things that they would have to learn about. They just hoped that they were capable. Chris had said that he knew that they could do it and so they too believed they could.

They started by making a list. Contractors, engineers, advertising agencies, network representatives, FCC bureaucrats; hundreds of people that they now needed, but had never had any reason to contact in the past. In fact, for the most part, they were people that Momma and Poppa had never had any reason to even think about before.

They found a young man who taught TV production

over at the University in Ames. When they had explained the project to him, they liked the way he responded and the fact that he didn't seem to look down on them as many of the others had. He legitimately wanted to help and he needed the money that they were offering to the production manager/producer. Others that they had interviewed were certainly willing to take their money and sign on to do the job, but they were condescending in their attitude, treating Momma and Poppa like a couple of lottery winning fools who were just throwing away their money.

They had run an ad in the *Wall Street Journal, Advertising Age, The New York Times* and *The Los Angeles Times*, as well as some smaller trade journals:

> *"Needed, skilled producer/director to create new infomercial targeting broad spectrum demographics offering respondents unlimited security and freedom. Newly formed company, financed through $77 million in lottery winnings. We have a concept. If you can turn it into reality, you are the special individual we are looking for. Please contact Security & Freedom Corp., Box 17, c/o this paper."*

Jack Stimson had never produced an infomercial. In fact, he had never even produced a commercial, other than those that he assisted his enthusiastic students with at the University of Iowa. When he first read the ad, he didn't give it a thought, but it caught his eye again as he leafed through the paper a second time. Although he didn't have the "real world" experience, he was very competent technically, and he knew that he could do the job. Further, he remembered reading about the old couple who had won the lottery and was intrigued by this new adventure of theirs.

By the best of his recollection, they had been relatively poor farmers prior to their big win. He wondered what they were like? What had inspired them to create an infomercial? What was their concept that would offer unlimited security and freedom to individuals in some new way?

87

So, he applied for the job and after a brief interview with Momma and Poppa, he was hired.

Once they met Jack, they longed to tell him the truth, but Chris had warned them to keep completely quiet about the real mission and in truth, they still remained mostly in the dark themselves.

Chapter 36

Al Goldman was sitting at his favorite table by the window upstairs at La Scala in midtown Manhattan. He had started the habit of taking staff members to lunch there three years ago. It was an easy walk from CBS headquarters at Black Rock, as the towering black stone CBS skyscraper had come to be known.

"You want to run that by me one more time?" asked Al with an incredulous tone. "Let me get this straight. You're telling me that some beautiful young blonde comes prancing into your office, you've never seen her before, she's not affiliated with any agency and she wants to buy 500 gross rating points a week for two months spread over three networks. This is all for commercials leading up to the Superbowl during which she wants to buy twelve two minute spots. Kid, I think somebody's putting you on!"

"Al, I'm not kidding, and there's more." Jim Weiss was dead serious. This was the biggest opportunity of his career since he had started selling TV time. He wasn't going to let Al belittle him or make him lose out on this opportunity.

"Al, listen to me. All these spots, which I agree are major overkill in reach, are designed for one purpose only: to totally saturate the market and achieve, as close as humanly possible, 100% awareness for a two hour infomercial which will run during prime time the Sunday following the Superbowl."

"But this is preposterous. Who is the target audience? Does she have any concept of how much money this will cost? What company does she represent anyway?"

"Al, the target audience is every man, woman and child alive. There are no parameters. It's everyone, and she swears that they have plenty of money, even though it is a brand new company."

Jim saw Al's eyebrows shoot up and quickly added. "The money's good alright. The company was initially funded by two lottery winners with $77 million dollars."

"Are they planning to run the infomercial on CBS?" Al was all ears now. He could see that Jim was not fooling around and had done his homework. He began to smell money.

"Not only CBS, but on all three networks, maybe cable too for all I know." Jim was improvising, Eva had said nothing of cable, but Jim knew that would get Al's attention.

"With that kind of buildup you're talking about, if the teaser spots and lead-up commercials are done properly, everyone in the country will be watching the networks. Why would anyone watch cable?"

Al realized what Jim had done and chuckled to himself. "This kid is learning the game."

Out loud he said, "Are you sure that they want to go to all the networks? Can't we convince them to stay with us? My God, with 500 gross rating points a week in paid commercials, plus the press coverage this is sure to get, plus the promos the network will do for free, one network would totally dominate the ratings."

Then, thinking out loud, Al continued, "Why in the world would they want to run the same infomercial on all the networks at once. Why not spread it around? By the way, how frequently do they plan on running this infomercial, and what's it about?"

Jim had hoped against hope that Al wouldn't ask these questions. He knew that as soon as he answered he would lose credibility. "Al, they're only going to run the infomercial once. That's why they insist on total awareness. As far as what it's about, the only thing I can tell you is that she said it's about attaining maximum security and total freedom. The company is even named the Security & Freedom Corp. SFC for short."

Al was back to skeptical again. "Why don't you tell me again who's behind all this?"

Al didn't really give a hoot as to who it was, he was back to being concerned if the money was really there to pay for the production expenses, plus air time for this cockamamie scheme. He'd seen every get-rich quick, financial security guaranteed, etc. infomercial that there ever was. He knew too, that some of the promoters had made millions, but he had never seen anything of the magnitude that Jim had just finished laying out for him, nor had any scheme seemed to make less sense.

"Remember the old couple in Iowa that won $77 million in the lottery a little while back, well it's them.

They own the corporation lock, stock and barrel, and they've backed it with their lottery winnings. Whatever their plan is, they're willing to gamble it all, or close to it, on this infomercial. Whatever they've cooked up, at least they must think it's pretty hot."

"What about this Eva, the one who brought the concept to you?"

"Al, I know nothing about her. All I can tell you is that she's as beautiful as a Hollywood starlet and she's convinced that this is the greatest thing since sliced bread. She's definitely new to the TV game, but she's got spunk and she's got money behind her. I wouldn't underestimate her. Look, she made it into my office and from what she said, I'm sure she's seeing all the right people at the other networks.

"Hey, the people at SFC may be crazy, but they have the money, and want to spend it. Al, I suggest we work as closely with them as possible so that we can get the biggest slice of this pie. The way I see it, we can't lose. We'll set the contracts so that the money is wire transferred from SFC's account to ours immediately after each commercial runs, the same with the infomercial. That way, no matter what happens, we have our money."

"Jim, Jim, Jim . . . slow down. If these people have the money that you say they have, then let's be careful not to offend them. After all this project just might, might, I repeat, be a success. If it is, we want to be right with them for the second round. Let's not upset them with less than an appearance of 100% support, at least in the beginning. If they show good faith, then we show good faith."

Al was obviously intrigued and with the amount of money involved, he had warmed to the subject considerably.

"This could be the biggest thing that happens in TV this year," he thought.

Chapter 37

Eva was excited. She was finally working toward something that truly made her feel good. Traveling to New York had been fun and exciting. The best part about it was that, although she knew practically nothing about TV, advertising, buying time or any of the media buzz words, it really didn't seem to make any difference. Once the network people determined that there was real money behind her, they bent over backwards to accommodate her.

It also helped that she was working with a drive and conviction the like of which she never realized existed. Her whole life was directed now, and the inner yearning, the thirst that previously could not be quenched, had been washed away in the tidal wave of belief and her faith that Chris knew exactly what he was doing, even though Eva herself didn't exactly understand it all. Eva was certain that she was now involved in the most important project of her life. A project that would impact not only her life, but that of all mankind. She often wondered why he had chosen her, but then she would just be glad that he did and not worry about it.

After speaking with Chris, Momma and Poppa had contacted Eva and invited her to join them, filling the dual roles of buying TV time and becoming the spokesperson for the Security & Freedom infomercial. Initially, she would be taping some of the commercials touting the infomercial and subsequently she would tape the two hour main event. Eva recognized that she was ideal for the role because of her looks and because she was well spoken. What she didn't realize was that probably her most important asset was her honest and heartfelt conviction. Eva had no idea what the script was going to say, but if Chris had helped Momma and Poppa write it, she knew it would be fantastic.

Every once in a while, Eva's mind would drift back to the hospital and the night that she made love with Chris while he was still a mysterious John Doe, and before she knew who he was. She now knew that back then he wasn't fully aware of his identity and was just beginning to gain awareness. She realized now that he was both a normal man and a great deal more, but that night in the still undeveloped state of the being that he was to become, he had been overcome by normal human desires. The result had been their joining which she had planned and orchestrated so well. As perfect as it had been, she knew that he had now grown way beyond the physical sex that both she, and he, had enjoyed together that night. His love was for everyone and was to be shared by the world. In this regard, she continued to keep the baby a secret from him. It would only slow him down in his mission which she believed would require every possible ounce of energy and concentration that he could muster.

Eva knew that she was now playing a role in the greatest act of love that could ever be committed. She didn't understand it, but she was committed to do her part to the best of her ability. She thought of herself as a small circuit in a highly complex computer. She was proud that Chris was relying on her. How far she had come from those sordid evenings in her past and the hopeless emptiness that had surrounded her life like a shroud.

Eva could not explain it, but when Chris had called and told her to leave the past behind and to open herself to a new and wonderful future, she was able to do so without any remorse or guilt about the past. In his way, and with his words, he had released her. She felt clean, fresh and renewed. "Born again." She laughed to herself as she thought about how she used to ridicule those born-again Christians whose holy roller TV sermons and tent ministries had seemed a circus to her, especially when one preacher after another was caught in compromising situations often related to illicit sex or money scandals, or both.

"This isn't like that," Eva thought. "This is the real thing. . . Chris really is going to change the world!"

She wondered what it was that was going to happen, but whatever it was, she knew it would be for the betterment of mankind including herself. Already, she was the happiest that she had ever been in her life. Even though she couldn't see the big picture, she was just happy to be doing what Chris wanted, and to be a part of it all.

Chapter 38

Paul Simons had been on the phone for about half an hour. He had known that he would hear from Chris, but he had expected the contact to be in person. Chris had explained about Momma and Poppa, the infomercial project, and without going into detail, had described the two hour infomercial as the single most important communication that mankind would ever receive.

Paul had a hard time believing it, but Chris told him that the $77 million that Momma and Poppa had voluntarily donated for the project would not be nearly enough and that in fact, Chris had only wanted to use that amount as the initial source of funds; seed money so to speak. Additionally, since the lottery winnings were public information, no one would question the availability of large sums of money that the Security & Freedom Corporation was willing to spend.

What each of the individual networks and agencies involved had no way of knowing was that the same contacts that Eva was making in the United States, were being made with every major network, in every developed country in the world. Chris had arranged for Evas in England, France, Germany, Australia, Canada, Mexico, Taiwan, Argentina, Israel, Norway, Turkey, Iran, Pakistan, etc., virtually every network in every nation was being approached.

In the Communist countries, where TV time was all government controlled, officials were being contacted, and if necessary, bribes were being made to assure that the air time would be available.

As Paul listened in awe to the magnitude of the project, he couldn't imagine how it could be accomplished either from a technical standpoint, or financially. Chris told Paul not to worry about the technical aspects, but the financial end was the area that Chris wanted Paul to handle.

Paul listened carefully as Chris told him that he would be transferring $300,000 from his account at Harrahs into three separate margin accounts, under Paul's name as an affiliate of SFC with three different stock brokers. He explained to Paul that over the next month he would be calling daily with various trades that Paul should execute.

Paul knew better than to question Chris, or bring up the risks involved in playing the market. He had seen firsthand what Chris could do and if Chris said he was going to make a bundle of money in the stock market, Paul was a believer.

The fact was that Paul was a 100% believer in Chris in every way. He hadn't reconciled in his mind exactly who Chris was, or even what he was. He knew that Chris was no ordinary mortal man and that Chris had an agenda for mankind that was universal in scope and beyond Paul's ability to comprehend. He wondered why he, a truck driver, had been selected to be part of Chris' grand plan, but he was delighted to be part of the team, and he was totally enthralled by his involvement with Chris. He knew that this was the best thing that ever happened to him and he was amazed that the agnosticism and cynical attitude that he had previously espoused so vehemently meant nothing to Chris. It appeared to Paul that all Chris cared about was the present and the future. The past was irrelevant to Chris as long as Paul was with him now in heart and spirit.

Paul had never felt so good. Like with Eva, Chris had chosen not to explain everything yet, but Paul realized that he was now involved with something that was bigger and more important than life itself. He knew that under normal conditions, what Chris was asking him to do would be laughably ridiculous, but with Chris, the impossible was commonplace.

Chris has told him that within 30 days, they would convert the $300,000 into $1.5 billion. Paul had no doubt that they would do it, even though he couldn't imagine how. One thing was sure, it would be fun trying.

Paul's first instruction from Chris, once the funds had been transferred, was to advise each stock broker to sell short Philip Morris, R.J. Reynolds, Liggett and Meyers, Brown and Williamson, and several other smaller tobacco companies.

The next morning after Paul had executed the short sales, headlines included a news release from the Surgeon General about the perils of tobacco usage; a reversal in the courts regarding a lung cancer victim who had sued one of the tobacco companies, where the appeals court had now found in favor of the victim; and finally a new major scandal involving previously unreported toxic chemicals in cigarette smoke that the tobacco companies had apparently known about for years, but had hidden from the public.

Tobacco stocks dropped like a stone. The triple whammy had started an avalanche that by noon had dropped the average tobacco stock by 50%, and in fact had pulled down the entire Dow Jones stock average by 7%. The overall drop was irrational as there was no real reason for the broad decline. . . no change in interest rates, or interest rate forecasts, no new fears of inflation. . . nothing. Even the tobacco companies had diversified into many other products for the specific reason of avoiding this type of precipitous drop on bad tobacco news, but the fact was that when the news hit, it darkened the mood of the whole market and traders began to run for the exits.

When Paul called his brokers at the end of the day, he learned that by selling short the previous day and buying in to cover the short sale at the new low level, he had effectively doubled the money, less brokerage commissions and fees.

With nearly $600,000 now available to him, he looked forward to Chris' next instruction.

Chapter 39

Murray Greenbaum read the reports over and over. Something big was going on; much bigger than he could have ever imagined. The question was, what to do? Murray had been extremely disappointed when Agents Aleo and Palmisano had followed up their premature, "we've got him," report with their more accurate, "we've lost him," follow up. But, as further tangential information began to filter in, Murray had realized that Chris was at the center of something extraordinary.

On-going stories on the old couple in Iowa had shown that from the day they met Chris, their lives had changed. They had not only won the largest lottery in Iowa history, but they had completely changed their lives. Incredibly, they were building a full-scale TV studio on the farm, complete with broadcast tower and the most modern high-tech equipment. They had applied for and already received a license from the FCC, and were apparently planning to do major cable TV broadcasting.

In addition, they had created quite a commotion on Madison Avenue, and among the networks, negotiating for air time to place saturation promo commercials on the air for some sort of infomercial that they were producing. The name of the corporation that they had formed for all of this activity was the Security & Freedom Corporation, and from what Murray could gather, their infomercial was about personal effort, or some "get rich quick" scheme. All he knew for sure was that they were committing huge sums of money.

These activities, very peculiar for a previously conservative retired farm couple, combined with the "coincidence" that it all began almost immediately following Chris' unexpected visit would have been enough, but now on top of everything else, Murray was beginning to see stories in the overseas press about SFC negotiating for huge amounts of TV time outside the U.S. as well. At first it was a report from the BBC, then TASS, then many others began to follow.

Then from another front entirely, reports began to come in from Wall Street about some unknown trader who had parlayed less than half a million dollars into over one billion in less than a month, and was on a roll the like of which no one had ever seen. When he saw the trader's name, Paul Simons, and when he saw that he was trading for SFC, Murray knew that if he tracked back, he would find that Chris was involved in some way. Sure enough it was a simple trace to determine that the original wire transfer into the first three brokerage accounts had come from Chris Lambert's account at Harrahs in Las Vegas.

Despite the fact that Murray had wanted to crack this mystery man on his own, the cat was now out of the bag, way out! Already there were investigators from the Internal Revenue Service snooping around. First as a result of Chris' surprise gambling winnings in Las Vegas, but now even more so that Paul was scoring huge on Wall Street with Chris' backing.

Every move that Paul made was perfectly legal, but he seemed to have inside information. He bought commodity futures the day before the U.S. Weather Service released new information regarding changing worldwide forecasts predicting a major drought which subsequently drove the price of soybeans and corn through the roof. He bought options in drug companies only days before the announcement of new miracle drugs. He sold liquor company stocks short just before Mother's Against Drunk Driving announced a new nationwide campaign against alcohol, unparalleled since the days of prohibition. The impact on all liquor-related securities was immediate and devastating. Once again, Paul's incredible "foresight" enabled him to almost double his investments overnight raising eyebrows from Wall Street to Washington.

IRS agents, SEC officials and now even FCC officials who had picked up on rumors that Chris was behind the new money that was pouring into the market purchasing TV time, now had their antennae up looking for anything that might not be totally above board.

Almost overnight, multiple investigations had been started. Although there was no apparent evidence that a crime had been committed, extraordinary things were happening, and everyone felt that something was awry. Each investigation led back to Chris, an individual who just appeared one day in a small town in Wisconsin. There was no history prior to his arrival there, and precious little information following his mysterious disappearance.

His fingerprints, which had been taken as a routine measure in an attempt to identify him, were nowhere on record. He had left the hospital without ever providing any background information on himself; no social security number, no past address, no work history, no nothing!

He had reappeared briefly and had been seen as he made his way out west to Las Vegas, but he had again dropped out of sight. The FBI agents in Las Vegas had tracked him down and thought that they had apprehended him, but instead had come up with some cheap hood who had apparently stolen Chris' rented R.V. The FBI had let the creep go, but later tracked him down in New York City where the only information that he provided was that a man with the same general description as Chris, had asked him to return the R.V. to Las Vegas. He claimed to have no idea where the man was headed or indeed who he was.

Murray had reported all that he knew to his superiors and was delighted when, because of the effort he had already put in, he was relieved of his other responsibilities and put in charge of a special task force with the sole purpose of tracking Chris Lambert down, finding out who he was, where he came from, and exactly what his relationship was to SFC.

They knew that there was something unusual, possibly extraordinarily special, about this man and Murray was given "carte blanche" in terms of funds available, and even offered military assistance, if required. Clearly the brass had become aware of some of the miraculous events, as well as the financial and media whirlwind that Chris was causing. They knew about it, but couldn't explain any of it.

Murray chuckled to himself, "the government doesn't like it when big things are happening beyond their understanding and especially beyond their control!"

In his many years with the FBI, Murray had never seen or heard of such a major investigation, or massive manhunt, authorized by the Agency for a man who, to date had as yet to commit, or even been accused of committing a crime.

Chapter 40

Eva had proven to be a quick study in the fast paced world of advertising and media buying. While the funds available appeared to be unlimited, she was working for a cause and made every effort available to buy the most premium time available with the greatest reach that she could. Her beauty and apparent naivete in the advertising world were disarming. Her negotiating skills, picked up from her previous experience in dealing with men, enabled her to lead them down the garden path, set her trap and then pounce. She was good, very good, and boy was she ever buying time!

Chapter 41

It was amazing what money could do. Momma and Poppa had known nothing about the world of business outside of farming. They knew even less about building a state-of-the-art television production studio and transmission tower. With the help of Jack Stimson and their lawyer, they had bought out a local TV station, in a matter of days, to facilitate their entry into the world of TV broadcasting. They didn't need the old studio since they were building a new one on the farm, but they needed the manpower and technical expertise that the station's personnel provided. Additionally, once they owned the station, it had greased the skids in cutting through all the FCC red tape required in terms of operating licenses, etc.

The new studio itself was more like a radio sound stage than a TV studio as it was designed for the sole purpose of videotaping the Security and Freedom infomercial which consisted of the simplest possible format; a presenter standing behind a podium as if lecturing to an audience.

Everyone involved was curious about the content of the infomercial, but despite the non-stop barrage of questions, Momma and Poppa kept quiet. There was not the slightest hint available to the ever-growing staff and crew.

Queries had also been coming in from the networks regarding the content. There were also constant reminders from their attorney that, although the SFC could contract for the time, nothing could be aired without prior review and approval by the network censors. Even the cable stations had to approve content, although their rules were much more lenient and flexible.

The truth was that Momma and Poppa couldn't reveal the content of the infomercial even if they wanted to. They simply didn't know themselves. Chris had told them that he would provide them with the script at the right time. In the meantime, once the studio and the staff were ready, they should begin to create a series of teaser commercials for the upcoming infomercial. The creative objective of the commercials would be to inform the target audience that the soon-to-be-aired show would have true

meaning for everyone.   Further, the commercials would
insure that everyone who saw them would understand that
the promise of the infomercial was guaranteed.   Every
man, woman and child who watched, would be positively
impacted from the standpoint of personal security and
freedom.   This was a rock solid promise and the teasers
were to get this message across.

The first commercial created was a very simple
format.   An authority figure, perhaps best described as a
combination of a loved father, a respected banker, and a
trusted doctor is standing on a cliff overlooking the ocean
at sunset.   He looks directly into the camera and, in an
authoritative, yet benevolent tone, he says:

> *"We are all certain that the sun setting
> in the west will rise in the east tomorrow
> morning. We are equally certain that the
> ebbing tide below will come back in a few
> hours to repeat high tide. The Security and
> Freedom Corporation, as a result of an
> unprecedented breakthrough for humanity,
> is going to absolutely and positively
> guarantee that every man, woman and child
> who watches at eight o'clock p.m. on the
> Sunday following the Superbowl, will find
> that their lives will be changed from that time
> on. SFC will unconditionally guarantee that
> their future security and freedom will be
> virtually insured forever.*
>
> *"This is not a gimmick, or a get-rich
> quick scheme. This, my friends, will be the
> opportunity of a lifetime. Your participation
> will be no more than to simply watch the two
> hour show. As hard to believe as it may seem,
> the entire course of your life will change as a
> result. It makes no difference, if you are a
> believer or a skeptic, rich or poor, healthy or
> infirm, young or old, employed or out of work.*
>
> *"We offer a breakthrough analogous to
> the creation of light where there was
> previously dark. I promise that you will not
> be, in fact, cannot be, disappointed!*
>
> *"Wherever you are, whatever you're*

going to be doing, please, please plan to watch. The world as you know it will never be the same. Your security and freedom will be as sure as the sun setting in the evening and the rise and fall of the tides."

Chapter 42

Paul knew the moment that he saw Eva that he was in love with her. A beautiful statuesque blonde with a very full figure, what his dad used to refer to as a "comfortable" body, and an inner glow, which was the dominant aspect of her first impression.

They were meeting in New York at Chris' request. Eva had told Chris that she needed a fairly large sum of money in certified checks to tie up a package deal that had opened up unexpectedly when another sponsor had canceled out of a Ted Turner deal with CNN. Chris had called Paul in his temporary office on Wall Street and Paul had jumped on a subway train to meet Eva at O'Henry's, at the corner of Madison Avenue and 51st Street.

He picked her out immediately. She was sitting at a corner table and stood to greet him as he approached.

"Hi, we meet at last," she said. "I guess it's about time that I met the guy who's been supplying me with all the money to make me a big shot from Madison Avenue to Hollywood."

She smiled as she reached out to him. He shook her hand almost mechanically. They looked at each other for a second, and then both broke out laughing at their formality.

"Sit down," she said. "We have a lot of catching up to do, but first, you do have the checks?"

"Yes. Here put them in your purse before I forget to give them to you."

"Thanks. Now tell me everything you know about Chris. Where did you meet him? Where did he come from? What's the infomercial all about? Tell me everything!"

Her rapid-fire questions caught Paul by surprise. He had assumed that Chris had told Eva everything and that he was the one who was in the dark. While Chris hadn't exactly said that he had confided in Eva, he spoke of her quite fondly and obviously he had a tremendous amount of faith in her. Nevertheless, based on her questions, it appeared that she knew less about Chris than he did.

"Whoa! Slow down. I think between the two of us, we may be able to piece some facts together, but before we do, let me ask you to answer one simple question. Although

104

you don't know a great deal about Chris, what is your overall impression?"

Eva didn't even stop to think. "He's the greatest man that ever lived. Don't ask me how or why I know because I can't tell you. I just know it and my life changed from the moment that I met him."

This sincere and frank answer was enough for Paul.

"Eva, I'll go first. I'll tell you everything I know, and then, if you like, you can do the same. I think that you and I are very lucky people to have been chosen to work with Chris and the more we help each other, and work together, the better off we'll be."

Eva really liked Paul. She watched his expressions and body language as she listened to him talk. She could see why Chris had chosen him. He was a man without pretense or false fronts.

Anyone else would have been astounded by what Paul told her, but Eva had learned to expect the unexpected from Chris and she listened intently as Paul told his story.

Later when Paul was finished, Eva told Paul about her relationship and experience with Chris. She left out nothing, except her pregnancy, and she found that he was such a sympathetic listener that she began to tell him about her background and the problems and hang-ups which had dominated her life prior to meeting Chris.

They were so enthralled with learning more about Chris and each other, that the hours sped by until Eva realized that, if she didn't rush, she would miss making the deal that Paul had brought the checks for in the first place.

She jumped up to leave and gave Paul a quick hug. She was surprised to find herself kissing him goodbye, but it happened so fast and so naturally, that she didn't have time to think. Then she had to run.

She laughed at the stray thought that went through her head, "did he notice that she was almost four months pregnant?" She guessed not because, although her breasts had grown substantially, her waist line was just beginning to expand, and, after all, he had never seen her before. Just why Paul's opinion of her was so important, she didn't know, but it was.

105

Chapter 43

Murray's task force had grown very rapidly once the IRS, the FCC, SEC and various other federal agencies had begun to question the activities of the SFC. While nothing ostensibly illegal had occurred, there was just too much money, too fast, from a company and people who had previously been entirely unknown and remarkably unprosperous. In each individual case that the task force was investigating, there proved to be only one common tie, Chris Lambert! In each situation, the individuals had lived unremarkable and divergent lives until meeting Chris. Then, after meeting Chris, their lives changed dramatically.

Momma and Poppa were poor retired farmers prior to Chris' visit. Subsequently, in less than three months, they headed up a fast-growing promotional company of some sort whose only product was a yet-to-be revealed two hour infomercial that guaranteed personal security and freedom. The new business was funded, at least initially, with the old couple's winnings in the Iowa State Lottery. Their first prize sum of $77 million, was the largest ever for the state and one of the largest in the entire country.

Incredibly, in only a few short months, they had exceeded the $77 million by purchasing a TV station, buying TV time, and in building a modern studio and transmission tower with all the state-of-the-art equipment necessary to broadcast worldwide through satellite link-ups. The additional money was coming in, as fast as they could spend it, from their affiliate, Paul Simons, a newcomer on Wall Street, who was already being called the financial guru of all gurus.

Murray was fascinated by Paul Simons. A trucker with a high school education, who had spent a week driving cross country with Chris Lambert, and very shortly thereafter had appeared on Wall Street. He arrived funded with money Lambert had won in Las Vegas, and once he started investing, had amazed the experts with his miraculous foresight, and uncanny stock-picking ability. It was almost as though he could see into the future.

Investigators had discovered that Paul had no previous business experience, and in fact, prior to his recent plunge into the market, he had never even owned a share of stock. In addition to the FBI investigation, the Securities and Exchange Commission was watching every move Paul made, joining the growing phalanx of stock and commodities traders who hoped to follow his lead. Never before in the history of the market had any single individual amassed so much money so fast.

The peculiar thing about it, that frustrated the investigators, was that there seemed to be absolutely no rhyme or reason to his stock picks. They all seemed to be entirely random except for one thing . . . they always went up, showing spectacular gains immediately after Paul bought them. This common factor, of course, was apparent only in retrospect. What no one could figure out was, how he was doing it. The SEC was dying to pin insider trading on him, but the fact of the matter was that he didn't seem to know anyone, or have any contact at all, in any of the companies or industries in which he was making a killing.

The only company that he seemed to have a contact with was SFC, and the best that anyone could tell, his relationship with them was simply as a provider of money. Once he had made it on the Street, he immediately transferred it to SFC back in Iowa. Despite the millions that were passing through his hands, he barely kept enough to eat properly.

The young woman, who seemed to be making all the media buying decisions for SFC was even more unlikely in her role than Paul was in his, if that were possible. She was responsible for having spent the largest portion of the old farm couple's money, plus a good bit more, which had come from Paul Simons' investments.

In an extremely short period of time, Eva was spending money buying media time at a rate faster than even the largest consumer-oriented multi-national corporations. Nothing in her background would have given any indication of her propensity for the advertising business.

She checked out as a farm girl from Wisconsin who, although somewhat of a loner, had nothing exceptional in her background as a young girl and teenager. Like many young women, she had decided upon a career in nursing. Here, her life path had taken a different turn. While studying to be a nurse at the University of Wisconsin, she had begun to lead a dual life. A perfect student by day, she, for some reason known only to her, had chosen to pursue a secret career as a call girl. Whether it was for the money, or for thrills, or possibly for drugs, the FBI investigators couldn't figure it out.

They determined however, that her secret life which continued long after graduation, had abruptly stopped shortly after Chris Lambert had been admitted as a John Doe, an unconscious and mysterious patient, at the Eden Prairie Hospital where Eva worked.

Interviews with the old farm couple, who insisted upon being called simply Momma and Poppa, were no more fruitful than the interviews with Eva or Paul Simons. In each instance, they freely admitted what they were doing, but were very circumspect in explaining how or why. Additionally, they did not hide the fact that they knew Chris Lambert. In each case they suggested that he had been the catalyst that changed their lives; however, they were all apparently bound by the same promise not to reveal the exact nature of their relationship with him.

If they knew who he was, where he came from, or any other details about his life, they weren't about to share them with the FBI or anyone else.

Eva's conversation with the FBI agents was fairly representative and showed how deep their affiliation with Chris was, yet was indicative of their reticence to explain it in any way . . . until the time came.

"When you ask me about Chris Lambert, you're asking me about someone who came into my life and changed it profoundly for the better; a change that will last forever. In many ways I was a lost soul who hungered for fulfillment, and never before had I met anyone who, simply by being there, was able to satisfy my every need.

"My involvement with Chris, Paul, Momma and Poppa, and many others, is the beginning of something that will be clear to everyone in a very short time. More than that, I cannot tell you, but, if you look at my life and how I have changed, you may consider it a portent of the future.

"You are curious about the money. You are curious about the infomercial. Your questions show that, because you don't understand what is happening, you have assumed that there is something wrong. This time

108

gentlemen, you are the ones who are wrong! Be patient, everything will be explained to you soon. I can assure you that nothing but good intentions are being fulfilled and that SFC is exactly what it says it is, a private corporation dedicated to bringing a new level of security and freedom to every man, woman and child on earth."

When Eva spoke, she exuded a glowing attitude that both agents interviewing her later referred to as a "certainty that went beyond self-confidence". Whatever was happening and whatever her role, there was no doubt that she was a true believer. They had never seen anyone with her degree of commitment to one individual, and they marveled at her complete transformation, after what appeared to be only a brief encounter at the hospital, followed later by communication apparently limited to the telephone.

Chris Lambert himself was an enigma. Despite months of intensive investigation and research, Murray knew no more about the man than he did the first day. They had managed to trace Chris' path from the hospital in Wisconsin to Las Vegas, and they had strung together a network of people whose lives Chris had touched. But who Chris was, where he came from, and what his motives were, was still a mystery.

Murray was intrigued, to say the least, about the incredible impact that Chris seemed to have on people's lives. He was further amazed at the actions of those same people after meeting Chris and the broad influence that those activities were having. The focus of which was SFC and the infomercial, which was being touted worldwide as the most important show ever to be produced. Yet no one seemed to have any details about it, other than the now famous undefined promise of security and freedom for all who watched.

Murray was starting to feel the heat from the top, as the Agency was getting pressure from the White House to find out what was happening. This new upstart of a company was now having a major impact on the world markets, and with the delicate balance of the economy possibly in jeopardy, the President wouldn't let the matter rest until he knew exactly what was going on.

Other than the fact that Chris seemed to leave a trail of inexplicable events, and people totally committed to him and the SFC "cause", Murray had nothing to report. Worse still, even with all the power of the FBI at his disposal, Murray didn't have a clue as to where Chris might have disappeared to.

Chapter 43

It was almost time. The air time had been bought and the lead commercials and teasers had been running on schedule. The response to the planned media saturation was greatly enhanced by the news media having picked up on the incredible amount of money being poured into ensuring worldwide awareness of the upcoming event.

Sharp reporters had also followed the trail of money backward from Eva, to the SFC, to Paul and his incredible string of home runs in the world of securities and commodities trading. It hadn't taken long for the press to discover that Paul's success was of recent origin, and that his initial stake had come from an account at Harrahs in Las Vegas. Simultaneously, the press had uncovered a growing investigation within the FBI searching for a mysterious individual named Chris Lambert, who had apparently appeared from nowhere, and subsequently disappeared without a trace.

When the press realized that it was the same Chris Lambert that had staked Paul Simons' entrance into Wall Street, the explosion of media postulation, supposition and stories, both real and imagined, was without parallel. To add fuel to the fire, the tabloids had begun to run stories about inexplicable miraculous events which seemed to follow Chris Lambert wherever he went. While the mainstream press refused to run this type of story, they were well aware of them and had begun to wonder if they hadn't been scooped by the tabloids, as the proof kept coming in with eyewitnesses and incontrovertible evidence.

Chapter 44

Momma and Poppa were worried. The network censors were really on their case. The last phone call from NBC was typical of all the recent calls.

". . . Look, I understand your problem, but with all due respect, if SFC is not able to provide a tape, or at least a script for the infomercial, then there is no way we can let it air. We realize the magnitude of this project, and the millions that have already been spent in promoting it, but, just like the other networks, our censors must see the infomercial before it airs."

Poppa had assured the man that they would get their tape in plenty of time, but the fact of the matter was, that even though they were ten days from air date, and despite the state of the art production studio, multi-million dollar transmission tower and complete studio team now on staff, there was no tape! In fact, to Poppa and Momma's knowledge, there wasn't even a script.

Chris had called them several times to reassure them. Each time, when they hung up, they once again had complete faith, and pressed forward with the hiring, the construction, and developing the commercials. The staff had been wonderful, and Jack Stimson, from the University, had proven to be an excellent choice as production manager. He really ran everything for Momma and Poppa. Gratefully, unbeknownst to him, he also acted as a buffer between those staff members who were curious about the infomercial, and Momma and Poppa. They had told him that for security reasons it was being kept very hush-hush. Only those who absolutely needed to know would be told, and then only at the last minute. However, as time passed, and they had no further direction from Chris beyond producing the teaser commercials, Momma and Poppa had no choice but to tell Jack something, so they had come up with a story that the infomercial was being produced secretly at another location. Jack was notably disappointed by this news, but he accepted it graciously and continued about the business of preparing and overseeing everything else very professionally.

At last everything was ready. Jack and the crew

were waiting with great anticipation the appearance and the first showing of the infomercial. By this time, Jack was privately a bit annoyed that Momma and Poppa had not had the confidence in him to allow his participation in the production of the SFC infomercial. In fact, although he had tried to do a little snooping, he was still totally in the dark. He, and the others, understood the importance of secrecy and the "need to know" policy that had been implemented, but Jack felt that his hard work, dedication and loyalty should have resulted in Momma and Poppa sharing with him.

At this late date, Jack was even beginning to wonder about the intelligence of the decision to hold the tape back from the censors until the very last minute. What would happen if, for some unknown reason, one of the networks were to pull the plug . . . it would be a total fiasco, and a financial disaster unprecedented in TV history.

Jack kept his thoughts to himself, but just like Momma and Poppa, he was worried, very worried.

Chapter 45

Chris was focused. He had become the center of the rhythms and pulsating colors. Time had ceased to exist. As God lives within every cell of our bodies, Chris was at one with eternity. While the flow of history had rolled before him, he recognized man's fatal flaw and knew what must be done.

The flaw, or what many describe as "original sin," was the remnant of base animal instincts. The instincts and emotions of "predawn" and early man had not changed or evolved despite the intellectual and technological growth that man had enjoyed as he passed into the modern age. Man's dilemma was that the early survival instincts, selfish egocentric forces that along with superior intelligence had enabled man to rise above other animals, had not changed. From these base instincts were born greed, avarice, jealousy, etc., that were the characteristics of modern man's penchant and potential for evil.

Unlike animals whose actions are driven by instincts and bodily needs, man is sentient. With his ability to reason came an understanding of ethics and morality and a recognition of choice between base instinct and that of morality. Man's religions often characterize or symbolize this internal struggle as the existence and influence of God, and the opposing influence of a lesser, but still powerful entity, the Devil.

In other words, every man knows his own standards, an understanding of right from wrong, but he also has the innate ability to choose which path to take and there is no guarantee that the "good" path will be chosen.

Religions created by man provided the opportunity for individuals to repent of their sins, turn away from their baser instincts and follow the high road with promised forgiveness. While this was predominantly an expedient rationale for people to put evil behind them, with the universal concept that it was better for bad people to become good, rather than stay bad, with no possibility of forgiveness, it really hadn't had much of a positive impact on man's actual activities.

No matter how many men had identified the right

114

path; no matter how many guidelines, rules or commandments; no matter how many promises that were made; no matter how many covenants with God; man was still the same, and essentially destined by human nature to continue to live in the misery caused by the heretofore irreconcilable dual nature of man; the intelligent being forever bound to the egocentric beast.

Chris would be the catalyst that caused the change replacing the baser instincts with an intuitive spiritualism which would allow man to comprehend the nature of things and man's role within the universal fabric. This realization would forever change man, eliminating evil and its paralyzing effect on society. Brother would no longer rise up against brother. Peace and harmony would prevail, and man's concept of Heaven on Earth would become a reality instead of a dream.

There were two ways in which Chris could accomplish this end. Both would have the same result, but for man, they would be very different. Chris could simply expand his radiant influence and inject the needed spiritualism into every man, woman and child on earth. In one cataclysmic instant, mankind would have changed. History would start over, and man would live in total harmony and grace. Man would "fit" into the universal pattern. He would be a perfect part of the rhythm of colors, in balance with the rest of existence, but he would no longer be man.

The unique quality of man was exactly the same as man's dilemma. Man had the ability to choose! If Chris simply injected spiritualism into mankind, and in a stroke, eliminated the need or ability to choose, what purpose would it serve? Man's struggle would have been for naught, and man's existence, to date, would have been meaningless. Far better for Chris to be a catalyst, an agent for change, who incorporated man's ability to reason, into the process. If mankind knowingly and willingly made the conversion, then man's prior existence and history would have had a purpose and truly been worthwhile.

Chris knew that for man to achieve fulfillment, he must follow the second of the two choices. Man would be a participant in the new future and would either reap the benefits of success or suffer the consequences of failure.

Chapter 46

"Chris! Thank God you called!" There was tremendous anxiety and tension in Poppa's voice. "I've held off the networks as long as I can. If we don't get them a tape of the infomercial, they're going to pull the air time. I'm not kidding. We're down to the eleventh hour."

Chris could hear the urgency in the old man's voice and he marveled at what this gentle elderly fellow and his wife, both way past retirement age, had accomplished. As people often did, they had lived up to his expectations and had done a fabulous job. In a sense, it had been unfair of him to keep them in the dark, but he had done so for their own protection, and to maintain the integrity of the mission that only he, and he alone, could accomplish.

"Poppa, there's been a change of plans. Rather than an infomercial, I'm going to appear live for the two hours."

"But Chris, the networks will never go for it. They've never even met you. They have no idea as to what you might say and even if the censors agreed, the lawyers never will."

Chris laughed, Poppa had sure learned a lot, and of course, under normal conditions, he was absolutely right. But these weren't normal conditions!

"Poppa, Poppa, slow down! We'll provide a written affidavit promising not to violate any network or station guidelines, or break any federal, state or local laws. Further, we will indemnify each and every station against any possible lawsuit and back it up with a personal surety bond for one billion dollars. The money will be held in escrow by a bank, or banks, which will be mutually acceptable to the networks, and, in fact, we will allow each network to have its own legal department draft its own language for the agreement and indemnification.

"If you have the numbers handy, I will be happy to speak directly to the powers that be, and we'll have this problem resolved today, and the paperwork signed tomorrow."

Poppa was relieved. As usual, there had been no reason to worry. Even the most insurmountable problem was child's play to Chris if he put his mind to it. He wished

116

he could be a fly on the wall in the network boardrooms when they received Chris' call. Poppa had never seen Chris fail to persuade people, and this would be no exception. What he was doing was unheard of, impossible under normal conditions, but Poppa was once again confident. He couldn't wait to relate this new turn of events to Momma, Jack Stimson, and the rest of the crew. After all, Poppa knew that Jack had put everything into the project without ever getting visibly angry about being kept in the dark, although Poppa knew that it had been eating away at Jack. Now there was no reason to keep quiet any longer, and Poppa was anxious to clear the air with Jack, whom he had come to think of as a son.

Chapter 47

Murray Greenbaum had never been so excited. Finally, he was going to not only find the elusive Chris Lambert, but he was going to see him first hand, and probably meet him, at the internationally awaited live SFC two hour program which was going to be telecast from Momma and Poppa's farm in Iowa. Murray had so many questions that he could hardly wait for the show to be over so that he could spend some time with Chris alone.

Murray certainly had not planned a trip to Iowa to watch the live program, but when he received a call from Chris, he leapt at the opportunity. Although he didn't expect any trouble, he had brought a cohort of agents with him, some obvious and others, the majority, undercover, just to keep a close eye on Chris, and all the goings on surrounding the broadcast. After all, this was the man that for months had managed to elude the FBI, while amassing the largest fortune in modern times, coincidental with creating the most talked about, and yet most secretive media event since the inception of television.

Murray had been shocked when Chris had called him.

"I understand that you've been looking for me."

"This guy sure is a master of understatement," Murray thought.

"I'm sorry if I've caused you any inconvenience," Chris said, "but I really wasn't aware that you were looking for me. Have I done something wrong?"

Murray was perplexed. How should he answer? The fact was that Chris hadn't done anything wrong that they knew of. He simply had done the impossible over and over. So much so, that the national media had Chris' various activities and involvements plastered all over the press, calling him everything from a miracle worker, to media genius, to stock market guru . . . the man behind Paul Simons' incredible string of successes in the various markets. Further, he had managed to disappear without a trace right out from under the eyes of the FBI, and now was claiming that he wasn't even aware that they were looking for him. After only the briefest contact with people, he had created the most loyal band of followers since the Pied Piper . . . but, the fact was, he hadn't, to anyone's knowledge, broken any laws . . . so how to answer?

"Mr. Lambert, we have been seeking you out, and I am delighted by your call, not because you are suspected of any crime," Murray hoped that the lie didn't show in his voice, "but because of your extraordinary accomplishments. The government simply wants to learn more about you"

"Are you going to watch the show?" Chris asked. "Because, if you are, all of your questions will be answered. Meanwhile, I can assure you that nothing I have done, or would ever do, would be criminal, immoral, or unethical in any way by your, or anyone else's standards. I also understand that you, and many others cannot believe what I just said. I simply ask that you watch the show, and then make your decisions. Afterwards, if you have any questions, I will be glad to respond."

Chapter 48

It was fifteen minutes to air time. All the satellite links were at the ready. The legal eagles and censors had all been satisfied by Chris' indemnification, and the nations of the world were tuned in, and waiting, with newscasters worldwide speculating on the message to be forthcoming from the now famous, yet mostly unknown, Chris Lambert, the brains and money behind SFC.

The world was riveted to the edge of its seat. How could this man, this company, possibly guarantee the entire population of the world, security and freedom for life . . . whatever he was going to say, the world was waiting, and it better be good!

Chapter 49

"Well, will you look at this Ben. Come in here and look at this!"

As Ben came into the TV room in their small home in Woodland Valley, Phoenicia, New York, he joined his wife as she stared at the TV. Ben had heard about the SFC two hour show, but a country born and country smart natural cynic, he had told Mary that it was just a bunch of hype for some "get-rich-quick" or insurance scam. But, when he came in and saw the TV, he was immediately certain that he had been wrong. This was going to be something different, something special.

What Ben and Mary saw on the screen was exactly the same image as was appearing throughout the world. They saw a young man, probably in his early thirties. He was dressed in worn high-top work boots, slightly faded Levi's, and a blue work shirt open at the collar. His hair was long and flowing. He was standing in front of a barren field with a brilliant sky behind him, that matched his intense, yet warm blue eyes. The young man's arms were raised in a V-shape as though he were drawing strength from the heavens. Surrounding, or perhaps emanating from his body was an aura of pulsating colors that mesmerized Ben and Mary as they watched. As he began to speak, Ben and Mary were transfixed as they first saw and then felt themselves become engulfed in the gentle rainbow that had magically extended from their TV set to surround them.

"My name is Chris Lambert. I must admit to you that I have brought you together to listen to me under false pretenses. The sole purpose of the creation of SFC, and the extensive advertising campaign was to create as large an audience worldwide as possible. For this subterfuge, I apologize, but I assure you that my message is of even greater import than advertised. Together, beginning today, we will begin to change the world.

"Please listen carefully to what I am about to say. This message is for all of mankind, but can only be received through each and every one of you individually.

"From the tiniest subatomic particle to the broadest expanse of the universe, we are all part of a whole which the human mind is incapable of understanding. The whole is like a fabric woven in intricate designs and patterns, each with a distinct and important meaning and purpose; some subtle, some plain and obvious.

"The intricacies and complexities of the human body offer only the least significant examples of the magnificent and purposeful organization contained with the totality of the entity called existence in which we all reside, both physically and spiritually.

"Time measures the distance between events, but is not constant. It expands and contracts even within our minds, as one event from the past seems like yesterday, while yesterday's occurrences may already be forgotten. Yet we look to time as a constant in remembering our past and planning for our future. We do not truly understand the concept of time any more than we understand the totality of our existence. Therefore, we ask ourselves: Why are we here? How long have we been here? How long will we be here? What is the purpose of life? Where did we come from?

"These are the tip of the iceberg of the mysteries of life that men will never truly understand. But, within man's grasp, are the answers to other dilemmas which have wreaked havoc with civilization and society from the beginning of mankind. It is these issues that I am here to address. As for the existence of man within the universe, I can only tell you that every speck of existence, past, present and future, is equally important. In the greater sense, the totality was in the past, is now, and will be forever; while the integral segments and systems may be in a continuing state of flux and change. The entity is constant and forever.

"My message must override and supersede not only your politicians and governments, but from this moment on, your entire way of thinking must change. Believe me when I say what you hear today will represent the beginning of the end of the world as you know it, or if not heeded, will be the beginning of the end for mankind.

"I am here as part of the natural order of things. What began as an imperfection in humanity has grown into cataclysmic proportions where something must occur to change the course of events. Some of you may want to consider me the 'Son of God,' a means of divine

122

intervention, and, in fact, as I have said, my existence came as a result of the need for such an intervention. I am, however, no more divine or spiritual than each of you. I come from the same source, albeit by different genesis, and I am a man with the thoughts, emotions, hopes, dreams and doubts, the same as any other man. I am different only in that I have experienced contact with eternity and I have been granted the gifts of knowledge and understanding.

"I have been sent to bring man back from the brink of disaster and into a harmony that will be in accord with the everlasting.

"You must listen carefully, as no one else can save you; not your religious leaders, or politicians, nor your government . . ."

Chapter 50

The phone was ringing in the studio office where Murray had been entranced by the incredible preamble by Chris Lambert. Murray could barely pull his eyes away long enough to glance over and pick up the phone.

"Greenbaum."

"Murray, this is the Director. I'm sure you've been listening to this lunatic. The President just called. He wants him off the air, and he wants him off now! Something very strange is occurring. We contacted the networks and told them to cut to a commercial, news or any damn thing, but they seem to have lost control. Whatever type of transmitter they have in that cockamamie farm studio, it seems to have its own satellite links, and the networks can't cut it off. There's no telling what this madman is about to say, but if the President wants it cut off, then by God, that's what we'll do. You got it? Whatever you have to do to stop that broadcast, do it! Murray are you there? You got it?"

"Yes sir!"

Murray hung up the phone. His adrenaline was pumping. He had always been a behind the scenes researcher and had never been involved in such an exciting investigation. Now, here he was, on site, with the Director giving him specific instructions. He would show them that he was the right man.

Murray was only about ten feet down the hall from the engineers suite that was controlling the broadcast. His men were scattered around the building, but Murray was sure that he could stop this himself. After all, he only had to walk down the hall, show his credentials, give the order, and the engineers would have no choice but to stop the program; or so he thought.

Murray glanced back at the TV, but although he was immediately drawn to it, and again felt engulfed by the strange colorful aura that had surrounded him since Chris had appeared on the screen, it did not prevent him from leaving the room and heading toward the broadcast studio.

All the engineers and technicians were fixated on the monitors above the panel. They barely noticed when Murray entered the room.

"Shut it off!" Murray shouted. "I'm special Agent Murray Greenbaum of the FBI," he said as he flashed his badge, "and I have direct orders from the President of the United States to shut down this broadcast."

The startled technicians looked up, but no one made a move. Perhaps the intensity of the rhythmic colors issuing forth from the monitors increased a bit, or perhaps it was Murray's imagination. For a fleeting moment, he doubted his own actions. After all, he of all people, knew that this Chris was no ordinary person, and as far-out as this all seemed, who could really be sure of anything?

Murray's training took over. He had been given a direct order, and directly in front of him was the means to execute it. He reached out to the biggest dial on the panel and spun it . . . nothing happened. The picture on the monitor remained crystal clear, and the audio was undisturbed. Like a mad man, Murray began to flip switches and turn dials with absolutely no impact on the screen what-so-ever. Now the technicians and engineers were in a total state of amazement. It was virtually impossible for the broadcast to continue uninterrupted with this going on, but there it was, totally undisturbed.

Murray looked bewildered. One of the technicians pointed toward the door to the outdoor sound stage which had a red light over it meaning that the stage was in use, and on air. Murray ran to the door, but it was locked. A sound proof steel door was too much for Murray to tackle, so he looked for another avenue of attack.

The phone rang. Murray grabbed it.

"What the Hell is going on?" It was the Director. "Why haven't you pulled the plug?"

Murray hung up the phone without answering. Of course, why hadn't he thought of it . . . pull the plug! All he needed to do was find the power panel and throw the main circuit breaker.

As Murray headed toward the basement, he heard sirens in the background, but he didn't think too much of it. He was too intent on his mission. He raced down the stairs and into the cellar, found the power panel almost instantly, and pulled the main lever. Nothing happened. He had expected the basement lights to go out along with everything else in the building, but nothing. He quickly threw all the small switches, even though he knew that once the main switch was thrown, the rest were irrelevant. Stunned, he slowly went back upstairs, turned into the first available office and lo and behold, the TV was still on, and there was Chris.

Murray sank back in the chair in the office. Maybe he'd better listen. There was something much bigger than he could have possibly imagined going on here. Bigger than him, bigger than the Director, bigger than the President; never mind his orders, Murray decided to watch. As he watched and listened, the rainbow of colors once again surrounded him, and he began to really listen to Chris for the first time.

Chapter 51

With no immediately available military base or National Guard unit on hand, the FBI had called the Iowa State Police as backup to Murray and his group. Initially, only called as a precautionary reserve force, the State Police had now been informed that the objective of shutting down the illegal and reactionary broadcast had now become their primary responsibility.

As if on cue, seven State Police cruisers all converged on the small parking lot at the recently built studio on Momma and Poppa's farm. With guns drawn, prepared for any response, they entered the studio only to find everyone seemingly transfixed by the charismatic individual on the monitor. Confused by the rainbow-like aura that seemed to emanate from the entire studio, they nevertheless broke down the studio door to the sound stage, and found themselves face to face with Chris, live and on the air.

Chris seemed neither surprised nor particularly disturbed by the sudden arrival of more than a dozen officers as they came smashing through the door with guns drawn and aimed at him. They, on the other hand, were more than disconcerted. They were stopped dead in their tracks by the appearance of the scene before them. Chris smiled and stepped toward them with an outreached hand that beckoned them to him. Simultaneously, the aura of the colors quickly engulfed the officers as they looked at each other, and then at Chris, with awe and amazement.

"My friends, do not be afraid. You are here due to misunderstanding and misdirection, well-intentioned as it may be. I simply ask that you join the others in listening to what I have to say. I know that you will neither harm me, nor stop me from my purpose because, if you try, you will find that you cannot. Your shotguns will not blast, and your pistols will not fire. Look closely, these weapons have turned to rubber in your hands. If you try to approach me, you will find that your legs will not support you. Therefore, relax and be comfortable, my friends, and listen, because what I have to say affects each of you equally.

"To those of you now watching TV who sent these

men, I request that you too rest comfortably and listen, for no matter what power you might exert to stop me, my message is more important and therefore you will not succeed. Just as these few men have been stopped and now sit with me in anticipation, so will anyone or anything.

"I am not here to prove anything, nor am I here to save you. The proof will only come from your accomplishments, and the saving must be by your own hand. Much of what I am about to say will appear to you as a bright lamp to a blind man. He can feel the warmth and can sense there is more, but he will never see the light itself, and all that it illuminates.

"If, through one world-shattering event such as nuclear war, the striking of an errant meteor, or the explosion of the sun, man were to be wiped out, the balance of the physical universe would not be effected. Man would have existed, and would forever hold a place in the space time dimension. Man's struggles with ethics, morality, and good versus evil would, however, merely be a footnote in the annals of time.

"Equally, would I be destroying man, if I were to reach out and touch the mind and soul of each and every individual on earth, eliminating the ability to choose between right and wrong; disintegrate the evil side of man, fulfill all of man's needs and at the same time, eliminate his ability to choose, or to make moral judgments. In so doing, I would be wiping man from the face of the earth as surely as if the earth were to explode.

"The beauty of man lies in his ability to choose, and decide; to inherently know and comprehend right from wrong.

"In the evolution of the human species, evil, which was an outgrowth of the self-centered animal survival instinct, remained because it acted as a stimulus, a catalyst for achievement; a counterbalance against which the forces of righteousness were always tested. A combatant is always stronger if he is actively challenged by his opponents. However, as mankind has leapt ahead with technological and scientific breakthroughs, which have not only improved man's living conditions, but have also created man's ability to destroy himself, man's emotional development, and inner struggle with right and wrong have not progressed.

128

"While there were practical needs for technical development, such as improving the human condition, feeding the hungry, and healing the sick, there has never been an imminent need for man to overcome evil. The penalty was always elusive and distant, while the rewards for evil were immediate. Greed, avarice and uncontrolled desire offered the possibility of instant gratification.

"Today, I am changing all of this. I am promising to each and every man, woman and child, that mankind has one generation, starting today, to make the change; to put evil behind and move forward in harmony, brother with brother, family with family, nations with nations; all religions, all races, all creeds, all political persuasions. There will be no second chance. Either man accepts on faith what I am saying and changes the course of human nature on his own, or in one generation, this opportunity will disappear forever, and the disharmony that is now inherent in the society of men will be forever eliminated. Man will no longer exist as man, but the grace and balance of existence in its entirety will go on as before.

"You, first of all, must believe what I say is true. You must believe in me, and you must believe that I have come to you because of your need. Further, you must recognize and believe that what I have said is incontrovertible. Everything is as I have stated, and no action that you might take, can change these facts.

"Secondly, recognize that you are all brothers and sisters. You always have been in the past, but have not acted accordingly. It is now incumbent upon each of you to treat each other with unconditional love, generosity and kindness . . . to treat each other as you would have them treat you. The logic of this golden rule has been known since time began, but now it must be incorporated into basic human nature, not by edict or fiat, or by my saying so, rather, because each of you finally and truly accept it as the only way. If everyone truly loves others as they love themselves, then evil will disappear from the face of the earth as does the darkness with the dawn.

"Today, this is a world of 'haves' and 'have nots,' with only the smallest percentage representing the 'haves' who control the wealth and power. My friends, I can assure you that these riches are fleeting, and that all the money in the world cannot buy what you can have

129

simply by replacing evil in your hearts with love, kindness and understanding of your fellow man.

"Be pure in your motives. Make peace among yourselves. If you follow the commandments of your heart, you will have done your share. Each individual has the capability of changing the world around him. Start with your families, your friends, your business associates, and if your heart is true, then your words and actions will spread like wildfire. Your message will be heard one thousand fold, as not only your words, but the examples of your deeds pass from one person to the next."

The State Police captain, now sitting entranced on the floor, looked up to Chris and said, "Who are you? With what authority do you speak? Are you saying you're a God?"

"Captain, I am a man like you. I am here because I am needed and the truth is my authority. I am no more or less a God than you or anyone else. While you may find it difficult to understand my origin, equally you cannot explain your own. Nevertheless, we are all here today, and we are part of an existence greater than any man could ever imagine. It is now time for us to grow up, to set aside evil and immediate gratification in favor of goodness and eternal sanctification."

"But, what will happen if we don't?" asked the Captain.

"In one generation, mankind will come to an end. How it will happen is irrelevant, but mankind as it exists today will disappear from the face of the earth."

One of the technicians who had been sitting along the side of the sound stage said, "You're Christ aren't you? You're Christ come back to give us another chance!"

Chris looked intently at the man. "In truth friend, Christ never left. Like me, he came to man because of a need. Then, as now, men knew right from wrong. You all know in your hearts that man has always known right from wrong. In a very real sense, Christ was a reflection of man looking at himself for answers. The answers had been there all along, yet even when they were spelled out, man refused to see the light, and turned a deaf ear on the eternal wisdom of righteousness.

"My message is not complicated, and I have endeavored to reach as many people as possible. Those of

130

you now watching this broadcast must take this message to those who have not seen or heard me this morning.

"There must be no exceptions. Within one generation, man must, by choice, eliminate evil, in all its worldly forms, from existence. I assure you that it is within your power to accomplish this, and it will be no more miraculous then man flying in space, breathing beneath the sea, or making life possible through the transplanting of vital organs from one person to another. All these things and many, many more, were virtually impossible less than a lifetime ago, yet now they are commonplace. The next generation must, in the same way, find within its hearts and minds a means to extinguish evil.

"Now, I'm sure there are many questions that you have. I have arranged for a direct telephone service into the studio, and will respond to your calls. Just dial 1-800-END-EVIL."

Almost immediately, the switchboard lit up.

"Why are we here?" the first caller asked.

Chris looked up and then directly into the camera. "We are here, because we are here. Our purpose is not to fathom. Rather, we must accept our existence at face value, and put every last bit of energy into it so that our time will not be wasted either as individuals, as a people, or as a civilization.

"There is no harm in conjecture or wondering why we are here, but we must not be overcome with frustration when the answer is neither apparent, nor forthcoming. We must believe that our existence has some importance and relevance in the greater scheme of things, but more important is how we interact with each other, and with the world we live in. Regardless of why we are here, can anyone argue that we are better off living in disharmony with ourselves or with nature? I don't think so. By simply accepting the fact that we are here is enough. What we do with our time here is the more important and relevant question."

"What happens when we die?" the second caller sounded frail, old and frightened.

"Do you remember where you were before you were born? Were you uncomfortable, unhappy, discontent? Did you suffer? Did you have hopes, dreams, expectations?

131

Were you even aware of your existence? The answer, of course, is that you were not, and therefore could not be troubled by worries and concerns. When you were conceived, the very beginning of perception and awareness in this new chapter of your existence began, and with awareness was the inception of your ability to determine right from wrong.

"Just as today, I have explained that man must find a way to eradicate evil from mankind as a whole, every individual has had the ability and opportunity to do so for themselves throughout the expanse of their lives. Every person whose whole life has been dominated by evil, may, during their last days, recognize evil for what it is, and change their ways. In the same way that I said that mankind would live on if evil is extinguished, an individual will continue forever if his life ends with the good having overcome evil in his heart. The natural harmony and grace of existence corrects flaws, and evil is one of those flaws.

"What exactly happens when we die, man is not meant to know. However, we can be reassured by the recurring cycles of nature that we see all around us. Just as the sun is reborn every morning, and the new grass and flowers come with the spring; just as we pass along our memories, our history and part of ourselves to our children and grandchildren; and just as we change the lives of everyone we touch, the world and everything in existence is affected in some way by our being. When we pass on, that impact is not forgotten or erased.

"After we die, we may go to where we came from, or to somewhere else entirely. There is no way to be certain. However, the mark that you make during this lifetime is under your control, and it is up to you whether this time on earth is worthwhile or wasted."

The lines were all blinking as Chris took the next call.

"What about God? Is there a God? Will praying help?"

"Wherever you are, just look around you," said Chris. "Look at the miracle of life and the wondrous beauty of nature. Consider the perfect balance, harmony and cycles of existence with the intricate and complex combinations of atoms, molecules, cells and species that

132

make up this earth. Look to the heavens, and to the crystal formation of a diamond. Think about where all of this came from and how it came to be.

"Just as you exist with no way to explain your being, so the universe with all it contains also exists with no explanation. The concept of existence itself is irrational without a proven origin. Yet, everything is here and does exist. It must have started somewhere.

"That was a very long answer which can be summarized by simply stating, 'Yes, there is a God.' The totality of existence is God's being, presence and purview. God is Father to us all, provides nourishment and shelter, and orchestrates the symphony of all things.

"Does prayer help? You are part of the existence of God. Prayer is first of all recognition of a need, and your prayer is a belief that your need should be met. Can there be a more powerful force than recognition of a need, and faith that it will be filled?

"With faith, anything is possible, because faith is the unconditional belief in the unprovable. Man will never know how, or why, or the true impact of prayer, but just as God exists in everything and everyone, prayer, in concert with a recognition of God's omnipresence and de facto omnipotence, not only works in the world, but also becomes a reality unto itself.

"Prayer breaks down the barrier that our inability to rationally comprehend God establishes. Through prayer, we can become tuned into the inexplicable, the irrational, the undefined, the miraculous. Prayer is our connection in a greater existence that we cannot possibly understand, but we can find comfort, sympathy and strength in.

"I would suggest that if you are looking for a formula for prayer, there is no better example than the Lord's prayer found in the Bible's book of Matthew. It was Christ's example of how to pray and represented His summation of man's relationship with God. Let us go through it together.

"'OUR FATHER,' He said, 'OUR' because everyone is included in God's embrace. He does not discriminate. 'OUR' refers to all mankind without condition or exception. Christ said 'FATHER', not Creator, or Lord, or Master, or King . . . but 'FATHER'. He could have used any of the other terms, but the message he gave to us was to consider God as the 'FATHER' of mankind, to be revered, respected and held in awe; to be trusted, loved, needed; to be unquestioned and believed wholly and completely as a child looks to a parent.

"'WHO ART IN HEAVEN.' 'WHO' gives us the sense of an individual, a person like us who we can relate to in our own terms. 'WHO ART IN HEAVEN' means that He is there. He actually exists 'IN HEAVEN.' If He is there, then wherever, or whatever 'HEAVEN' is, it exists, and is a real place, be it physical or spiritual, that the faithful can look forward to.

"'HALLOWED BE THY NAME.' This is a straightforward unmitigated acceptance, belief and endorsement of the unique holiness of God.

"'THY KINGDOM COME,' by using 'THY' in describing 'KINGDOM', Christ is identifying heaven as God's domain, and that mankind can only be received there by God's grace. 'KINGDOM' meant the same thing 2,000 years ago, as it does today. A king has unlimited power and control over his realm, and the people therein, as God has over the world and everything on it; heaven and everything in it; all things we understand, and all things we are yet to know and understand. When He Says, 'THY KINGDOM COME', it means that God's 'KINGDOM' is everywhere. It was in the past, is now, and will be in the future. The 'KINGDOM' is there for all who are able to accept it.

"'THY WILL BE DONE,' states a desire to follow the Ten Commandments, the Golden Rule and all those things we know in our hearts are right. Once again, there are no modifiers, no exceptions. By praying, 'THY WILL BE DONE,' we are saying that we want what God wants, and we pray that His goals be met.

"'GIVE US THIS DAY OUR DAILY BREAD.' We are calling upon God to watch out for us and care for us. It is recognition that we exist by the grace of God, and we look to Him to provide for our needs.

"'AND FORGIVE US OUR TRESPASSES.' As we have already discussed today, it has always been man's nature to falter, trip up, err, . . . sin, and by asking forgiveness, we recognize our failure and show our repentance.

"'AS WE FORGIVE THOSE WHO TRESPASS AGAINST US.' If we can forgive others, then God can forgive us.

"'LEAD US NOT INTO TEMPTATION.' By admitting and

recognizing the temptation for what it is, the prayer itself will help us to avoid being tempted.

"'AND DELIVER US FROM EVIL.' When we ask for deliverance, we are recognizing God's omnipotence; that He can and will, if we ask and believe, take us away from 'EVIL', any 'EVIL', no matter how powerful. Christ identified the existence of 'EVIL'. Then, as now, 'EVIL' existed; but then, as now, if man truly wanted deliverance, he would not be left behind.

"'FOR THINE IS THE KINGDOM, AND THE POWER, AND THE GLORY, FOREVER AND EVER.' The powerful words ending the prayer are both a reminder and a reverent reidentification of the domain, omnipotence and potential for eternal joy that God represents in His relationship with man.

"So you have asked, 'Does prayer help?' The answer is yes, and while the concept and existence of God may be impossible to understand, it certainly is not difficult to believe, and it is that belief, belief in God, and your existence as part of His realm, that empowers you and makes you strong."

The fourth caller had waited a long time. "Why are there so many religions? Is one of them right? What about organized religions versus personal faith?"

"There are as many possible interpretations of God's existence as there are human beings. None of them are right, and none of them are wrong, because it is truly beyond man's understanding to comprehend an omnipotent, omniscient, eternal being that encompasses everything that has existed from the beginning of time. Even an expression such as, 'the beginning of time,' shows the inadequacy of our language and ability to relate to the nature of an eternal entity. Therefore, each of us in our own way must come to grips with this dilemma. Leaders emerge and common thoughts develop into organized religions. Often divergent in their practices, the fundamentals all come back to the same central theme reflecting man's struggle within, the battle of good versus evil.

"Religion, whether organized or individual, is a good thing if it is helpful in overcoming the darker side of man. As a result of our conversation today, some religions may grow, while others decline. The important thing is

135

the message, and that message is to each person individually. Choosing to bond together for moral support, teaching and discussion may help some, and yet be meaningless to others. As in all things, the choice is yours."

The next call took a different turn. "Is there intelligent life elsewhere in the universe?"

"My friends, intelligence is everywhere. There are as many kinds of intelligence as you can imagine, times one thousand. Right here on earth, there are a multitude of examples of different types of intelligence. A colony of ants, or a swarm of bees, are examples of communal intelligence, where each individual makes up a part of the whole, and the community itself is the intelligent entity. Plant life has a quiet, yet not entirely passive nature. A tree reaching and bending for maximum sunlight, or a cactus sending down deep roots with many tendrils spreading out and searching for water are examples of genetically implanted instincts, representing intelligence of a different sort.

"Our tendency is to define intelligence in our own terms, but the fact is, that where there is existence, there is life in some form, and with life, there is intelligence; some more advanced, some less. Throughout all existence there is only one constant, and that is change. Change is universal, and it is fear of change that acts as an impetus to the learning process. The more we know, theoretically, the more we can predict change, and the less we have to fear. That is why you ask the question about intelligent life elsewhere. You are hoping for a clue as to what the future might bring. Unfortunately, just as the concept of God and eternity are unfathomable to the human mind, so is accurate prediction of the future.

"Again, I say, focus on what you know, and what you can change. If you do, the future will take care of itself.

"In short, yes there is intelligent life elsewhere, some that you can perceive and understand, and some that you may never even encounter, but YOUR intelligence is what's important. Use it effectively in making your judgments and setting your direction for the future. One generation will come and go very rapidly. Do not waste it!"

"Why did my uncle die so young?" The seventh caller was upset. "He was the most wonderful, most generous man I ever knew. He never hurt a soul, and yet he died of cancer and suffered terribly at the end? If we are to believe that good prevails over evil, why did my uncle have to die?"

"I can feel your pain, and I know that everyone has these same thoughts and questions from time to time as life deals out a seemingly unfair blow to them or their loved ones.

"Is not death the ultimate threat, the single event most dreaded and least sought after? Yet, may not death be the ultimate reward? Can we who do not even understand our own existence, question, or even recognize, what the real impact is of that which we perceive as bad, only because it is unknown, versus that which we perceive as good.

"As for pain and suffering, remember, only those who have suffered can truly appreciate joy; only those in pain can know the meaning of release. Perhaps it is precisely those who suffer the most that we should envy, for they, more than anyone, can appreciate the little things. How many of us go through life barely aware of others and the wonderful things around us. We take so much for granted, and appreciate so little. I cannot explain the reason for every hurt and every illness, but I do know that in every life there is a purpose and a reason, sometimes easily understood, others incomprehensible.

"Do not dwell on what you cannot understand, but accept things as they come. Your uncle served as a fine example for you and others whom he touched in his life. He left behind a rich legacy of goodness that will now have been heard by millions of people. His pain and suffering were not in vain, nor were they punishment. They were just a part of his life, part of the role that he played in man's struggle. Be proud of your uncle, do not grieve for him. Live up to his example, and you too will shine in the new world to come."

"Why are there so many poor people, and so few wealthy, and why do some people work hard all their lives and remain poor, while other simply inherit such wealth that, no matter how they squander it, they still have plenty to pass along to the next generation?"

The eighth caller had touched upon an area that Chris had expected. It was a question that had bothered man ever since the beginning of civilization.

"First of all, let us remember that man enters the world with nothing, and leaves with nothing. Whatever worldly goods a man may possess, they are not his forever. He simply has use of them for a brief period. Secondly, is not the poor man often happier than the rich man? Without the burden of possessions to preserve and protect, does not the poor man better have the opportunity to reflect on what is truly important; family, relationships, bettering oneself, and the world around him.

"It is not wealth that should be envied, rather, it is the spirit of the man. If a man is of good spirit, and willingly shares what he has, gives of himself, is he not truly wealthier than the miser who hoards his stocks and bonds hiding his wealth behind guarded walls so that it won't be stolen? Isn't the poor man who walks the street without fear better off than the rich man who travels in a bullet proof limousine, surrounds himself with body guards, and is constantly in fear of being robbed or kidnapped?

"Is not the poor man who finds true love from an equal woman, better off than the wealthy man who casts off wife after wife, always searching for the younger, the more beautiful? In his old age, which will be happier, the poor man surrounded by his children and grandchildren, or the rich man whose divorces and infidelity leave him lonely and alone to be comforted only by paid servants and mistresses?

"My friend, wealth comes to some, and not to others, but it is not the wealth itself that is important. It is what you do with what you have. It is who you are, and how you treat those around you. Life on earth is fleeting, and each of you may judge for yourselves which is a better legacy, the influence of a good man on family, friends, and acquaintances, or the burden of wealth left as the only record of a life dedicated to possessions."

The ninth caller was truly in a dilemma, and Chris could hear the frustration, and the suffering in his voice.

"My wife has been hospitalization for a long time, and the doctor says that there is no chance for recovery. She neither knows, nor recognizes me. In fact she has no idea of who or where she is. I have fallen hopelessly in love with the woman who has cared for my wife for years, since the beginning of the illness. This woman, a widow, has come to love me as well. My priest says that I cannot divorce my wife while she lives, and I don't want to commit adultery. What shall I do?"

"You must do what your heart tells you is right. If you were to switch places with your wife, and it were you in the hospital bed, and it were her with the lover, would you accept and bless her relationship? If so, then you know the answer to your own question.

"If, on the other hand, a young man recently married to a devoted and loving wife were approached by a young divorced secretary in need of consoling and found that their relationship had gone past comforting to sex, but rationalized that it was okay since the young woman truly needed him, and his wife would never know, then to this, I would say 'Grow up!' When you must try to fool your own heart and mind, you are headed in the wrong direction, and the result is always guilt. Guilt is a negative emotion that helps no one, and can always be foreseen. It usually follows thoughtless actions, selfishness, and childish succumbing to the desire for instant gratification.

"The guidelines and rules of your church were established by that church for the good of all members, but only you can know and judge what is right and acceptable for you."

"I am poor, and my family is hungry. Yet there is wealth all around me. Is it so wrong for me to steal what I need for my family? Don't the wealthy people steal from the poor by overcharging for goods and underpaying for labor?"

"I shall answer your first question for it is a good one, but I will disregard your second because you must not rationalize what you do, and your judgment of right and wrong, by what others do around you. What you do yourself is what is important.

"Just as the unbidden rain falls from the sky to water the flowers and the trees, and just as the sun rises, unbeckoned, to warm all living things, so you too must trust in the very nature of existence to provide for you and your family.

"Man is not an animal that simply takes what is available wherever and whenever possible. We recognize the rights and privileges of others, as we expect ours to be

139

recognized.   Every society has developed laws and traditions that support these mores, but again, it all starts with the individual.   Since you would not want others to steal from you, it is impossible for you to justify your right to steal from others.

"Although life may be difficult, the struggle that you are facing will make you and your loved ones stronger, and the family bonds that you are now building, will last forever.

"One final question, I have for you.   Would you rather have your child know you as a thief, or as a poor man with pride and honor?   Which memory would help your children raise their children?   By the way, the same answer goes to the individual who wants to rationalize lying or fraud due to poor circumstances.   Like stealing, they simply cannot be justified."

"What about war?"

This last caller, in one three word sentence was questioning the morality of the single activity that had the greatest impact on the direction of human life since the recording of history.

"Life is precious.   There is no more miraculous event than the creation of new life through the joining of a man and woman.   To destroy a life is wrong.   There is no situation under which the taking of another human life is justified.

"Wars are the macro result of man's inability to control evil.   While it is true that in any war, just as in any disagreement, there may be a right side and a wrong side, the taking of lives is never the answer.   Man has within him the ability to overcome evil through determination and self-control.   When man accomplishes this end, wars will cease to exist.

"I can see that there are many more calls, and many more questions, however, I cannot stay much longer.   I have given you the message that you must take to heart. One generation will pass as the blink of an eye.   However, I will leave you with one last word of encouragement.   It is within your power to accomplish this seemingly impossible task.   Evil can be overcome by man in the short span of a generation, and I assure you that no miracle is required.   The miracle already exists.   It is man himself.   It resides within man's ability to choose."

140

Chapter 52

When Chris stopped speaking, the rainbow of colors which had emanated from his body, and captivated the audiences worldwide holding them spellbound in their seats while they watched, suddenly disappeared.

In front of TV sets everywhere, people shook themselves as if recovering from a drug-induced trance, and looked at one another questioningly.

The police at the studio, suddenly realizing that they were now free from their invisible bonds, stepped up to Chris. About to handcuff him, they were confused and hesitated a moment. The message that he had given was clear and universal. Each of the officers knew that he had been speaking directly to them, yet they were under orders.

The Captain held up his hand, "Hold up." With a glance at his men, they stopped. "I don't think there is any need for handcuffs. Mr. Lambert, would you mind coming with us?"

As they led Chris away, there was an incredible scramble going on at every network, every affiliate, and every cable station. No one knew exactly how it had happened, but one thing was for sure, Chris Lambert had appeared on every station, and every channel of every TV set in the world. They would later learn that the broadcast was heard in the language of the people listening, which, in retrospect, was to be considered no more miraculous than the broadcast being transmitted from a studio where the power had been turned off.

The network news anchors and commentators were trying to rehash what Chris had said as he was led off to the Captain's police cruiser. Just as he was about to climb in the back seat, a shot rang out, and blood burst from Chris' chest where a bullet had entered and lodged in his heart.

Chris' last words, "Remember, only one generation!" were to be the headline of every newspaper in the country and around the world the next day.

Chapter 53

Eva and Paul had grown to know each other quite well during the months leading up to the broadcast. She had given up both her secret life and her nursing to work full time for SFC buying TV time. He had parked his truck for good, and had been living in Manhattan trading daily on Wall Street, with Chris' guidance, accumulating funds to support the entire endeavor.

Chris had spoken with each of them many times individually, and often together, along with the others who had formed as part of the SFC support team.

Prior to the broadcast, they knew that Chris was more than another mortal man, and that he had an important message for mankind, but he had given them no inkling of exactly what he was going to say, or the earth-shattering implications of his message.

They had agreed to watch the presentation together, and although they were probably more prepared than anyone, they too had watched the end of the broadcast in a state of awe. More than anyone else, they felt the shock when they realized that Chris had been shot, and they felt the greatest loss when they realized that he was truly dead. They simply couldn't imagine why he had allowed it to happen. He must have known, and surely he could have prevented it, but he didn't . . . they would never know why.

Eva had told Paul about the baby when it was impossible for her to hide it any longer. They both agreed that it was best to keep it a secret from Chris until after the broadcast. This had not been difficult since no one knew Chris' whereabouts, and his communications were entirely by phone.

In the months following Chris' death, Eva and Paul grew closer and closer together. The significance of Chris' broadcast was still a topic of daily news shows, sermons and dinner table conversation. However, with time, the immediacy and urgency of his message seemed to become more distant, and the miraculous aspect more interesting, as scientists tried to explain all the inexplicable events that had been a part of Chris' brief but spectacular life.

Eva and Paul met frequently with Momma and Poppa, as well as Jack Stimson and others who had been personally touched by Chris, and who were certain that mankind had better heed his words. Their efforts to rally support were only briefly interrupted when Paul and Eva got married in a small ceremony attended by the remaining SFC faithful.

Although she was 8-1/2 months pregnant, Paul saw Eva as the most beautiful bride in the world. Together they awaited the birth of the baby with great expectation.

Eva had gone into labor two days before the expected birth date, and fortunately Paul was with her to drive to the hospital, and to be at her side during labor. The delivery went without a hitch, with nothing unusual happening, except that right at the moment of birth, everyone in the delivery room thought they saw the slightest aura of a rainbow surrounding the little boy . . . but as quickly as it was there it was gone from sight.

Eva looked at Paul. Then they both looked at the baby.

The doctor said, "What are you going to name him?"

"His name will be Jesus," they both said together, and they knew that there was hope for the next generation.

Chapter 54

"Please fasten your seat belts and remain in your seats until the captain signals that it is okay to move around the cabin. We'll be taking off in just a minute, so sit back, relax, and enjoy your flight to New York. Thank you for flying Intercontinental Airlines."

Seventy years old, tired and discouraged, Jay sat back in the big jetliner seat anticipating take-off, and frankly glad to be on his way leaving Los Angeles behind. While he didn't look forward to the 4-1/2 hours flight back home to New York, he was very upset that this last meeting with the Ecumenical Council of Church Leaders had been such a failure.

"My God," he thought, "if after all this time, we can't even get agreement among church leaders, with petty jealousies and constant bickering over details impeding forward progress on the issues, then how in the world can we ever expect mankind to treat one another with brotherly love, share in what is good, work together to overcome evil, and live life putting aside political differences, geographic separation, racial conflicts, greed, avarice, hatred . . ."

Jay's mind was going a mile a minute. He knew it wasn't healthy for him to get so upset, but it was such a disappointment. His entire life's work had been dedicated to the seemingly simple proposition encompassed by the concepts of the brotherhood of man and living by the Golden Rule. Inherently, he knew that in the end, good would will out over evil, and in his early years he was certain that, through his efforts and others like him, a new beginning could be a reality during his lifetime. An accomplishment that his generation could provide to the future that would be a boon to all generations to come.

He was not looking to create a Utopia, for that was an unattainable dream. There would always be problems. Throughout existence, there were hurdles to overcome. Nature itself was stimulated to grow and improve each species by placing obstacles and hardships in the path of progress, thereby ensuring that the strongest, smartest and most adaptable would rise to the fore. No, he never thought man could achieve a utopian existence. But since his belief in the basic tenets of what had come to be known as the Lambert Challenge was so strong, he just couldn't understand why the rest of his fellow man, and especially those who professed to be deeply religious, didn't fully embrace these fundamental concepts.

Deep in thought, but bone tired from the trip and endless rounds of unsuccessful meetings, Jay began to drift off to sleep with these unsettling thoughts on his mind.

THUNK! It was a heavy, very solid sound. Jay awoke immediately with no idea whether he had been out for two minutes or two hours. It was the kind of unusual and unexpected noise in an airplane that instantly makes your palms sweat, and alerts your senses to whatever might be coming next.

Jay listened carefully, looked around, and used his entire body to determine if there was a change in air speed or altitude. Yet he could detect nothing. The only noticeable response to the noise was that a hush had come over the cabin. Eyes were darting this way and that with curiosity and a restrained fear that lurked just below the surface.

Sitting next to the window on the left-hand side of the aircraft, Jay looked over the empty center seat at the face of the man sitting on the aisle to his right. Unlike Jay who was an infrequent and sometimes timid flier, this man was clearly a seasoned traveler. This had been obvious by the way he had immediately settled into his seat, ignored the flight attendant's safety announcements, taken paperwork out of his briefcase, and had lowered the tray table to work within seconds after take-off.

The man's brow was wrinkled from concentration as he looked around, obviously as disturbed as Jay by the loud and unusual sound.

The noise had occurred no more than three minutes after take-off, and Jay thought it strange that neither the captain, nor co-captain, nor anyone from the flight crew had made any announcement about it. One of the flight attendants was walking briskly from the rear of the plane toward the cockpit with a determined expression, when the man to the right of Jay held out his hand, and in effect, blocked her way.

"Miss, what in the world was that noise? I've flown a lot in my time, but I've never heard anything quite like that before."

The flight attendant, trying unsuccessfully to hide her concern, said, "Nothing to worry about sir. I'm sure the captain will be on the intercom shortly to explain. Unfortunately, we are not permitted to comment or discuss anything of this nature until the captain has made his announcement. Meanwhile, please excuse me, but the head flight attendant has signaled all of us to the galley, and I really must get up there."

As the flight attendant made her way up the aisle, the man turned toward Jay to look out the window. Jay could see his eyes widen at what he saw. Jay turned to see for himself, and he immediately saw a heavy gray mist flowing out of an outlet on the wing creating a long stream that appeared to be about two feet in diameter stretching back behind the plane as far as the limited view from the small cabin window would allow Jay to see.

Jay turned back to the man next to him and said, "Sir, you look like you fly a lot. Do you have any idea what that is?"

"Jet fuel. That's jet fuel. Whatever that noise was, something has happened and the captain has decided to abort the flight and make a quick landing. Since the plane is loaded with enough fuel to fly from L.A. to New York, plus a cushion for safety, it's too heavy to land with the tanks so fully loaded. So, he's dumping fuel."

Jay was impressed with the man's knowledge, and nodded for him to continue.

"This happened to me once before on a Lufthanza flight out of Kennedy to Munich. We had a problem and the pilot did exactly the same thing. Nothing to worry about really. These pilots are well-trained, and know what they're doing. Whatever the problem is, he's apparently decided that there is some sort of risk, and we're going to go back rather than continue."

Just then the pilot came on over the intercom, "Hi folks. Sorry to report the inconvenience, but I'm afraid that the turn that you're just now beginning to feel is the plane turning around and heading back to Los Angeles International Airport. Some of you may have noticed that we have been releasing fuel ever since the loud noise that you heard shortly after take-off.

"Unfortunately, we had the rare and unlikely

146

experience of encountering a large flock of birds and apparently took several into the intake manifold of the starboard engine. We're not sure, but we think the instantaneous result was severe overheating and rapid seizure of that engine. We think that it was a thermal creak that we heard caused by the sudden intense heat as the engine stopped suddenly. The noise was metal reacting to the change in temperature very similar to the pings and banging you frequently hear in old homes as hot water hits cold pipes. Just as these sounds can be very eerie, but there is nothing to be concerned about, in this case there is no need to be alarmed either.

"Let me assure everyone that this jet has two other engines that are functioning perfectly. Both the co-pilot and I have been trained to fly and land this plane with one engine down. In fact, you probably noticed that other than the sound that you heard, the flight was uninterrupted in terms of speed or altitude as the on-board computer instantly compensated for the loss in power.

"Nevertheless, for obvious safety reasons, and in compliance with FAA regulations, we are returning to L.A. As a precaution, there will be fire engines and paramedic vehicles that will meet the plane out on the runway. Please don't be alarmed. They are simply safety measures required by the FAA during an unusual or non-standard landing."

The captain's voice was calm, measured and reassuring. There was a brief hesitation as the captain apparently looked at his gauges, and then he continued, "Please remain in your seats with your seat belts fastened until we are safely at a standstill at the gate. We should be back on the ground in L.A. in less than five minutes. We are currently at 6,000 feet making our approach, and should be on the ground shortly. Thank you, and once again, sorry for the inconvenience."

Reassured by the captain's remarks, Jay was nevertheless astonished to see that the man on the aisle was back into his paperwork as though nothing had happened. Jay looked around and he was somewhat relieved to see that others on the flight were not so blase.

Some of the passengers were anxiously glancing back and forth at each other. Some stared straight ahead, and some had their eyes closed as if in prayer. Jay noticed a woman three seats behind him on the right side of the plane clinging tightly to her infant baby as she stared straight ahead with an ashen color on her otherwise expressionless face.

Jay wasn't exactly scared. The captain's message had the desired calming effect, but he was still very tense. His earlier fatigue was gone and adrenaline was still surging through his veins. He suddenly realized that his hands were tightly clenched onto the armrests; so much so that now he was consciously aware of it. He could feel the sweat in his palms and an ache in his arms, from the tightness of his grip, that extended all the way up to his shoulders.

"Hey c'mon, relax," he thought to himself, "everything is going to be alright."

But everything wasn't going to be alright! Suddenly, without warning, the plane pitched forward and down beginning a fast hard roll to starboard. There was no announcement from the cockpit, and the panicked expression on the flight attendant facing him, seated on the jump seat across from the galley, only confirmed what Jay already sensed immediately. Something was wrong, terribly wrong!

Almost instantly, Jay felt the increased pressure on his back as the plane plunged and accelerated straight down.

The first reaction by the passengers was a deathly silence as incredulously they began to comprehend the events which had just occurred which were so contrary to the captain's controlled discourse of just moments before. The plane was obviously out of control and destined to crash within seconds. The still was quickly broken by a surging roar of hysterical screaming and crying.

Jay was surprised to find that he was having the opposite response. He felt somehow detached and distant from the uproar in the cabin. Inexplicably, time slowed down for him, and suddenly he was withdrawn into a world inside his mind totally undisturbed by the real life nightmare going on about him.

Chapter 55

Eva and Paul Simons had watched their baby very carefully to determine if there would be any unusual manifestations resultant from his secret lineage which was known only to them.

Although he was an active, precocious, and obviously very bright baby, there was no indication of anything special, unusual or abnormal. The pediatrician told them he was normal in every way, and by the time he was two years old, even Eva and Paul stopped looking for signs of his, for lack of better word "supernatural" parentage.

It was about that time that they decided to keep the identity of his true father a secret, even from him, and to bring the child up as their own natural child. It would have been different if he had shown any special or extraordinary mental or physical characteristics, but to both their disappointment, and in another way, their relief, he was just a little boy, no more, no less.

They promised themselves that they would fully expose their son to the teachings of his father, and wondered if he would have any unexpected reaction to watching the video tape of his father during the now famous infomercial.

Both Eva and Paul had been deeply saddened by the death of Chris Lambert, their mentor and spiritual leader, and they lamented the fact that he had been killed before he had an opportunity to do anything to implement the changes that would be necessary to meet the incredible challenge that he had extended to the next generation.

Initially, they had hoped that Chris' baby would become the natural leader of the spiritual revolution that Chris had envisioned. However, as little Jesus grew and developed with no evidence of any unusual powers, they indeed began to hope that he would not mature into anything more than the darling boy that he was. In fact, it was about age two, that they began to call him Jay in an effort to facilitate his acceptance among his peers as he grew older. They realized that they had named him Jesus while the fervor that Chris had created in their lives was still at its peak. Now, although they were still absolute and firm believers, they felt that Jay was a more appropriate name, for the time being anyway.

They felt somewhat foolish, and in a way symbolically disloyal to Chris as they made this decision, but they were both practical people, and knew that if they insisted on calling their son Jesus, it might cause his peers, and even other preschool parents to wonder. After all, once Chris had died, they had settled into a typical suburban existence with neither the wherewithal nor the desire to be leaders in a movement started by Chris and in which they had been prime supporters.

They lived their lives according to the principles that Chris had espoused, and set an example for their son, friends, neighbors and acquaintances. However, they simply didn't have the evangelical ardor which would have been necessary to carry on Chris' work in any other way than in their personal sphere of influence, and by their individual example.

After Chris had died, the Security and Freedom Corporation all but disappeared. Momma and Poppa had withdrawn back to the farm and were unwilling to deal with the publicity surrounding the extraordinary events that had occurred at the now boarded up studio which they had built. They had set up a trust with the money that was left over, the objective of which was to support equally any and all organizations established for the purpose of spreading Chris' message and meeting the challenge of the generation. Within a year, there were so many cults, communes, splinter groups and religious factions placing demands on the funds, that the income available to each became meaningless. Momma and Poppa as trustees became disgusted and decided to split the principle among the many splinter groups and be done with it.

For those who had been close to Chris such as Momma and Poppa, Eva and Paul, it was almost unbelievable as the world seemed to distance itself from Chris' message as time went by. Rather than concentrating on what he had to say, pundits, newsmen, analysts of current events, historians, and even theologians had begun to dwell on the vehicle rather than the message.

The focus had become, "How had he done it?", rather than, how to respond to his challenge and appeal. The miracle of the rainbow induced fixation, the simultaneous multi-lingual broadcast, the "impossible" broadcast with no power source, the network's unexplained loss of control; all of these things had been revisited over and over. The further that time took them from the inexplicable and amazing reality of the event, the more "rational" explanations there were. Hidden power sources, mass hypnosis, satellite boosters, simultaneous translators . . . there were theories and so called plausible answers for the entire event.

While there remained groups of believers that made it their evangelical mission to meet the challenge of the generation, the mainstream churches chose to simply ignore Chris' warning, and continued to operate just as before. After all, they rationalized that they were already preaching the word of God, and regardless of the sect or denomination, each in its own way was sure that they were on the right road toward salvation.

Only those few who had truly taken Chris' message seriously to heart believed that in one short generation, unless all of mankind were to effectively and forever put evil behind them, that everyone would feel the impact of Chris' warning. Chris had not been specific regarding the result, but the message had been crystal clear . . . "or change will be made for you, and mankind as you know it will cease to exist."

Chapter 56

Jay, again aware of his surroundings, saw the terror in the eyes of the businessman in the aisle seat next to him. Without thinking and without any explanation for his actions, he reached over, grasped the man's hands, and said, "It's O.K., don't be afraid. Everything's going to be alright."

Jay was surprised at his own words, and he was equally taken back by the calm and tranquility with which he spoke them. Indeed he was not afraid, and somehow in his serenity he had, with just a few words, quelled the terror in this stranger's eyes.

"I know," the stranger said, "it's going to be alright."

Jay then looked behind him at the woman with the infant. She was now staring straight ahead in mortal fear, squeezing the baby tightly to her breast. Jay caught her eye, and in an instant the unspoken message was received. The abject fear released its death grip on her and she smiled as she leaned down to kiss her baby goodbye.

Less than five seconds had passed, and as Jay imagined the earth coming up to meet the plunging aircraft at a rate of speed now exceeding 600 mph, Jay again drifted, losing contact with his immediate surroundings.

Chapter 57

Jay was walking up the gravel track that led up from the paved road which wound along following the meandering path of the valley stream. He had been down at the swimming hole with friends when he remembered that he had promised his mother that he would be home by 3:00 p.m. to watch the baby, so that she could go out and run some errands.

A thoughtful and conscientious 12 year old, Jay felt badly that he had almost forgotten to go back to the cabin. He hurried quickly up the steep hill at a pace that would have had an adult huffing and puffing in no time. Jay and his friends from the other cabins in the summer colony ran up and down the hill all day long, and his young body was so conditioned to the hill that he didn't even feel the exertion. In fact, as he climbed, he was struck by the awesome beauty of the Catskill Mountains. He had climbed this hill hundreds of times, and had been exposed to the view over and over, but for some reason this was the first time that he really saw it.

The majesty of the mountains and the spectacular beauty of nature suddenly overwhelmed him. For an instant, he forgot the urgency of getting back to the cabin, and stood still in the middle of the gravel road absorbing the enormity of the breathtaking panorama surrounding him. As though the thought had been percolating in his subconscious, and for no particular reason chose this moment to bubble to the surface, his mind leapt to the connection between the video tapes of Chris Lambert's infomercial, his parent's teachings, the church, the existence of God, and the undeniable, overwhelming and incomprehensible power of the Creator. His mental leap to comprehension was instantaneous, somewhat analogous to staring at a seemingly meaningless artistic pattern that requires the eyes to focus somewhere beyond the surface in order to identify the image. At first, it appears to be no more than a random pattern, and then suddenly the mind recognizes the right focal depth, and the previously unseen picture becomes crystal clear.

This moment, which came to Jay totally by surprise, would impact him for the rest of his life. He felt a kindred spirit with Chris and recognized that Chris had been speaking directly to him, not in exclusion of others, but directly to him, because he had been one of the ones able to "tune in". It was as if the signal had always been there, but up until now the receiver had been turned off. Now that it was on, Jay felt a new joy that he had never experienced before. He also now felt a new maturity and sense of direction and meaning that he knew he was destined to fulfill.

Chapter 58

The jetliner captain had years of experience and had been trained to remain calm even under the most traumatic and unexpected circumstances. At the current altitude and rate of descent, he knew that the plane would hit the ground in approximately 15 seconds. While his mind was grappling with this appalling fact, his hands and feet were moving with extraordinary speed following emergency procedures that he had practiced over and over in training, and were now automatic.

Nothing was working! The problem had gone way beyond the loss of power in the starboard engine. For some reason the hydraulic system had ceased to function, and he had lost control of both the rudder and the ailerons. The on-board computer showed no warning lights or signs of malfunction, and computer driven emergency compensation measures were not occurring.

Still professional and calm despite the clear and obvious disaster about to befall his plane, his passengers, and his crew, the pilot, suddenly detached, wondered if the flight data in the black box would provide enough information for the FAA and the airline to determine exactly what had happened to cause the total and complete loss of control.

He had no delusions of anyone living through this crash. He knew this would be a total wreck, with no survivors.

Chapter 59

Jay's mind jumped from his revelation on the gravel road to a dream that he had just after his 13th birthday.

He was sitting in an open area at the top of a cliff on a mountain top that was bare except for a few short scrub pines which had forced themselves up through the boulders. It was a place that he had been to many times since his father had first made the climb with him to this scenic lookout when he was 11. He had heard that it was one of the most beautiful lookout points in the Catskill Mountains, and he believed it as he viewed the green woodlands below, his eyes wandering up and down the valleys and looking down on the lesser mountains below.

In the dream, Jay watched a great hawk slowly circle scrutinizing the valley below for prey. The hawk was circling at about the same altitude as Jay's mountaintop perch, and as the bird swung around in great arcs, Jay was so fascinated by the primal beauty of this magnificent predator that he failed to notice the figure that sat down across from him and was silently watching him as he in turn watched the hawk.

The man broke the silence. "The hawk is so intent on what is below him that he is totally unaware of our existence. Yet, when he circles by he is close enough that we can see the shine of his feathers, the gleam in his eye, and the ready sharpness of his talons."

Jay, startled, looked over and saw a man sitting on a rock smiling at him. The man was perhaps 45 with a slight graying in his long flowing hair. He exuded confidence and warmth. Jay, who under different circumstances might have been afraid of the sudden appearance of a stranger, felt a sense of kinship with this man.

Sizing him up, Jay saw that he was a big man, perhaps a little over six feet tall, maybe 200 lbs., and that he appeared to be quite fit. It was only the gray in his hair and the beginning of age lines in his face that gave any indication of his age. Jay thought that he recognized him, but couldn't quite put his finger on where he knew him from.

"Who are you?" Jay queried.

"I am your father," the man replied.

156

"No, you're not! My father is Paul Simons. How can you say that you are my father?"

"Because I am your Father. In a way, I am also your father's Father, and your mother's Father. I am the Father of this generation and every generation preceded and every generation that is to come."

The word generation provided the spark which caused Jay to recall the fact.

"You're . . . you're Chris Lambert aren't you?"

"Yes I am."

"Why are you here? How are you here? You're dead. You died before I was born!"

"I am here to tell you that I am your Father, as I am the Father of all things. I am here to remind you that the destiny of mankind rests on your generation. I am here to ask you to reflect on what is important; to measure your successes in terms of relationships rather than things. I am here to encourage you to follow your heart and not be deceived by the false gods represented by pride, greed and materialism. There is no more satisfying endeavor than reaching out to another human being, helping in time of need, comforting in time of sorrow, sharing with those less fortunate, forgiving those who are less forgiving.

"Do not measure your success. Take each day and each moment as a precious individual instant in time that you either use toward total fulfillment, or waste forever. Every moment, every thought, every action stands alone and will not be blemished or tainted by previous mistakes or wrong doing.

"Look upon guilt as a worthless emotion with no positive impact or value. Do not feel remorse as a burden, rather, when you err, as all men do, use remorse as a stepping stone to bettering yourself. Wallowing in self-pity only sets a bad example for others and like guilt has no redeeming virtue.

"You have yet to experience the love of a woman, the death of a friend or relative, the birth of your own child. Your experience with the best of life, and the worst, is still ahead of you, yet you are old enough to understand intellectually. Be prepared as you enter into maturity for disappointments, temptations, joys and delights. It is your destiny that you will encounter the full range of emotions from ecstasy to heartache, for that is the destiny of every

157

man. Through it all I ask that you stay on the path that I have laid out for you. In so doing, the challenge of the generation may be fulfilled.

"Look at the hawk, see how he has spotted his prey and soars toward it with talons outstretched in confident anticipation. He has no doubts or second thoughts. Though he may miss his target four out of five times due to the swiftness of his prey, he will always return to his vigil, circling and reattacking with total confidence again and again. Failure is not part of his thought process."

Jay watched as the hawk swooped down and arose from the earth triumphantly with a crippled muskrat in his talons.

Jay looked back, but to his astonishment, Chris was gone. In the dream, Jay lingered there awhile on the cliff trying to incorporate Chris' new message into the matrix of beliefs that he already had.

The dream drifted off into black and then on further into awareness. Jay was back on the plane, plunging toward disaster. In real time, less than one second had passed while Jay's subconscious had recalled the dream. Once again, as if his mind were consciously avoiding reality, if that were possible, he was again back in his boyhood.

Other than the time on the gravel road when he felt he had a spiritual encounter with creation, and the dream in which he met Chris on the mountain top, Jay had only one other experience that made him question his origin and destiny. Throughout the rest of his life, he had experienced the same doubts, concerns, fears and inability to comprehend the multitude of questions that faces mankind. Yet, it was these three occasions that created within him a special knowledge and drive that enabled him to be a leader in the Lambert Challenge.

Perhaps it was the third experience that moved him the most. Yet at the same time, it was the most frustrating as he felt that for a moment in time, he had the power to reach out to his fellow man and tangibly change the attitudes of those around him. The source of his frustration was that the sensation had been ephemeral and fleeting, and the impact short-lived as he did not know where the power had come from, and he was unable to sustain it.

It was the custom in his church to have the minister welcome the graduating confirmation classes into the fold by the laying on of hands in the front of the church in full view of the entire congregation. The minister, the Sunday School teachers, and the assistant minister would bring each of the confirmands up individually, have a laying on of hands, say a few words of praise and welcome, and then move on to the next. It was a ceremony that created an emotional bonding and unity that frequently brought tears to the eyes of the young people as well as the teachers, and often the congregation. Tears or not, virtually everyone felt the warmth and emotional glow that only the physical touch of human and spiritual sharing can offer.

When it was Jay's turn something different and unique occurred that neither the ministers, nor the teachers, nor the congregation were prepared for.

As each of the individuals reached out and touched Jay, they felt an unanticipated and unforeseen, but very tangible radiance that flowed from Jay's body into theirs. In the past, both the ministers and the teachers had identified Jay as someone special in his Sunday School and confirmation classes, but it was not until this moment that they realized how special. None of them had ever experienced the spiritual and emotional response that they now felt. They couldn't define it and neither could Jay, but he felt it along with them and shared their amazement.

It was is if this physical contact with Jay suddenly put them in a total state of peace with an impenetrable barrier between them and anything evil. It was a never before felt sense of exquisite calm, strength, tranquility and support all wrapped into one invisible and inexplicable force that emanated from the boy's body.

The experience was so powerful that the minister forgot the familiar words of confirmation that he had voiced thousands of times over the years. The small group just stood there enraptured while the congregation itself became hushed as they realized something special was happening.

For a brief moment, Jay felt that he was the source, the leader that these people, indeed all of mankind needed so badly. Momentarily he felt empowered to respond to the challenge that Chris Lambert had made to his generation

14 short years earlier. In that moment, he felt he had the knowledge, the ability and the power. This was not conceit or ego. For that moment, in his mind, it was factual. It was at that instant that he fully accepted the personal responsibility to lead his generation into a new world free from evil and hatred, and the misery that they cause.

As suddenly as the radiance had appeared, it was gone. The ministers, teachers and congregation were left wondering what had happened, but Jay was left with an overwhelming dilemma. He had totally accepted the leadership role in meeting Chris Lambert's challenge. He had physically and spiritually felt in touch with the power necessary to accomplish his goal yet as quickly as the power had come, it had vanished. It would be Jay's lifelong disappointment and mystery that the unexplained radiance and power that he felt momentarily on his day of confirmation, never returned.

It was with these thoughts in mind that Jay once again became aware of his surroundings, and again, he could hear the panicked shrieks and wailing of his fellow passengers.

Jay could now see the tree tops, and he closed his eyes waiting for the impact regretting that he had not been more successful in creating the brotherhood of man that Chris had envisioned. He was surprised that the emotions created by a lifetime of apparently meaningless effort, and ending in disappointment could be felt as fully as he felt them now in what was both an instant and an endless moment all at the same time.

He was not afraid, rather he was resigned and saddened by the fact that he would die without having made any perceivable progress in meeting Chris' challenge. Subconsciously he realized that his death symbolized the end of his generation, and with it would die the hope for the future of mankind.

Ironically Jay realized that he would never have the opportunity to finish, but mentally he felt a comfort in reciting his favorite quote from the Bible.

"The Lord is my Sheppard, I shall not," Jay closed his eyes and readied for the end as his mind began to repeat the beginning words of the 23rd Psalm, "want. He maketh me to lie down in green . . ."

Chapter 60

Jay knew the impact would come any second. Curiosity, even on the brink of disaster, caused him to open his eyes for an instant and look out the window. He saw branches and knew that this was it! He shut his eyes tightly and involuntarily his entire body flexed in preparation for the impact and inevitable explosion to follow.

As the plane hit, there was an explosion of colors, but to Jay's amazement, he heard no noise and felt no collision. At the moment that the plane should have met the ground an explosion of an unexpected sort had taken place. It was as if the plane had been a laser beam of light that suddenly hit a prismatic barrier that upon impact had broken the beam like a spectrograph into every color imaginable. The light was so bright and intense that Jay could see the flashes through his eyelids. At first he thought it must be the fireball of the plane exploding, but then he realized that he was still alive and unharmed.

Incredulous, Jay opened his eyes and found himself along with the entire plane passing through the most astounding swirling rainbow of colors that one could ever imagine. The plane seemed to have entered a supernatural kaleidoscope that was spinning at tremendous speed.

Jay looked around the cabin. All the other passengers seemed to be frozen into place. There was no sound, nor any movement. Whatever position they happened to be in when they entered this indescribably beautiful whirlpool of colors, they remained in. Jay was somewhat perplexed by the fact that he appeared to be the only one that was awake and aware of the incredible events that were taking place.

He was so awe struck by the beauty of the colors that he didn't question what was happening. By all rights, the plane should have hit the earth and exploded seconds earlier, but it obviously hadn't. Nor did he have any doubts or thoughts that perhaps he was dead, and that this spectacular light show was somehow a part of his passage from the living.

No! Jay knew that he was still alive, and he knew

that he was now into something far beyond anything that he had ever had the capacity to comprehend, or to even imagine. All he could do was to watch breathlessly as the vibrating rainbow of swirling spectacular colors continued to draw the plane and everyone in it further and further into what Jay could only describe as an infinite and endless sea of prismatic beauty.

Then, as quickly as the colors had appeared, they were gone.

Jay was stunned. He looked around the cabin.

The woman with the baby was saying, "There, there, it's okay, just a little bump. Mommy's here. It's okay. Hush, hush, don't cry." She held the baby, rocked it in her arms and comforted it as only a mother can.

Jay noticed that the plane seemed to have righted itself back onto an even keel and he saw that the flight attendants were unstrapping their seat belts, and beginning to move around the cabin as if nothing more unusual than a bit of bad weather had occurred.

The captain came on the intercom. "At this time, I am requesting that the flight attendants please retake their seats, and all passengers remain seated with seat belts fastened and tray tables in the upright position until we have safely come to a stop at the gate.

"We are now on our final approach to Los Angeles International Airport. Once again, I'm sorry that in-flight difficulties required that we return to Los Angeles, but I'm sure that you will all agree that it's better to be safe than sorry.

"Thank you again for flying Intercontinental. Ground personnel will be awaiting our arrival to assist you in rescheduling your flight to New York. Thank you."

Jay looked around. Everyone was fastening their seat belts, stowing their tray tables and making final preparations for landing. No one but him seemed to be the least bit aware of the death-defying plunge that the plane had been in, or the inexplicable impact into the sea of colors in place of instant death that only minutes before had seemed to be the only possible outcome of an inevitable crash.

The businessman next to Jay was still working. Even though he had put up the tray table, he was using his lap and a magazine as a desk. He seemed intent on finishing one last memo prior to landing.

Jay shook his head and blinked. "What in the world is happening." He had verbalized his thoughts unintentionally, and the businessman looked over at him.

"You don't fly very much do you? Don't worry, everything is fine. The captain will land this bird so smoothly on the two good engines that you would never even know that anything were wrong. They'll have us rescheduled and back on our way in no time. We're just lucky that we're flying out of L.A. where Intercontinental is based. They have lots of equipment there and I'll bet they have us heading toward New York again within an hour."

Jay just nodded. How could he have been the only one to have experienced the past few minutes? He was certain that this had been no dream. The rainbow of colors had been so vivid that they would be forever embedded in his memory. No, this was no dream, but what had occurred, he had no idea. He decided, however, the best thing to do for the moment was to keep quiet. Obviously for some unknown reason, no one else on the plane was even aware of the miraculous shared experience that they had just gone through.

As the plane landed, Jay realized that the businessman had been right. There was no perceptible difference in the landing even though one of the three jets was not functioning. Jay let his mind dwell on this to avoid thinking about what had just occurred.

When the plane came to a halt at the gate, the passengers calmly and patiently arose from their seats, took their belongings from the overhead racks, and moved slowly down the aisle toward the exit. Jay followed in turn as if in a daze.

Since he was not expecting anyone to meet him at the gate, he looked neither to the right nor to the left as he deplaned. He just walked straight ahead. Out of the corner of his eye he saw a familiar figure standing back away from the crowd watching him. When Jay turned and looked over, the man signaled for Jay to come over to him. Jay realized instantly who it was, stood still with an incredulous gaping stare for a moment, and then slowly approached the man.

There was no doubt about it. It was Chris Lambert!

The hair, the face, the overall appearance . . . it had to be, but how could it?

Chris appeared to be about 45, and had not changed at all in the appearance from the time that he had appeared in Jay's dream some 57 years earlier when he had spoken of the importance of relationships over things, and had identified himself as Jay's father and in a larger sense, the Father of all men.

No, here he was in the flesh, standing in the L.A. airport gesturing for Jay to come over. Jay felt as if he were in some sort of dream, yet he knew that this was real. Just as he knew that the indescribable and unexplainable experience on the plane had been real.

"Welcome Jay. Welcome to the New Beginning. I know that you are totally confused, but the explanation is fundamental and simple as the truth always is.

"Since the world that you just left was populated by a mankind that simply could not overcome its evil and sinful nature, that world has ceased to exist, or perhaps better said, from this new standpoint, it never did exist.

"You are the sole inter-dimensional link between that world which, now might have been but never existed, and the New Beginning, to which you have now arrived and which has always existed."

"But how?" Jay couldn't understand.

"Come with me. There is a small chapel here in the airport. I'd like you to read something which may help you to understand."

Together they walked to the empty chapel and sat down on one of the back pews. Chris pulled a slender book from the rack on the back of the pew in the front of them and handed it to Jay. Jay saw that it was entitled The Holy Bible, and wondered for a moment at its slim dimensions.

"Turn to Genesis and read Chapter 3."

"But, for what purpose? I have read those passages many times as they speak of man's first sin," said Jay.

"Please, Jay, bear with me. You are no longer where you were, and things are no longer as they were. Please read this brief passage, and it will provide you with an insight into this world that you have entered."

"Now the serpent was more crafty than
any of the wild animals the Lord God had

164

made. He said to the woman, 'Did God really say, "You must not eat from any tree in the garden?"'

"The woman said to the serpent, 'we may eat from the trees in the garden, but God did say, "You must not eat fruit from the tree that is in the middle of the garden, and you must not touch it, or you will die."'

"'You will not surely die,' the serpent said to the woman. 'For God knows that when you eat of it, your eyes will be opened, and you will be like God, knowing good and evil...'

"When the woman saw that the fruit of the tree was good for food and pleasing to the eye, and also desirable for gaining wisdom, she took some and ate it. She also gave some to her husband, who was with her and he ate it. Then the eyes of both of them were opened, and they realized they were naked; so they sewed fig leaves together and made coverings for themselves.

"Then the man and his wife heard the sound of the Lord God as he was walking in the garden in the cool of the day, and they hid from the Lord God among the trees of the garden. But the Lord God called to the man, 'Where are you?'

"He answered, 'I heard you in the garden, and I was afraid because I was naked; so I hid.'

"And He said, 'Who told you that you were naked? Have you eaten from the tree that I commanded you not to eat from?'

"The man said, 'Oh Lord forgive us, we were both tempted, and we ate from the tree. The serpent coaxed us, but it was not the serpent's fault; tempting is his nature. Lord, we knew better than to break your commandment, yet we were weak and succumbed. We now have knowledge that was forbidden to us, but we have also learned remorse. We ask for your forgiveness and for divine guidance as we make choices in the

165

future.'

"The Lord looked upon his creation and smiled. He said, 'You know that there will always be temptation, and in your frailty you will always be weak, but with remorse comes forgiveness, and with forgiveness, redemption.'

"Now that you have eaten from the tree of knowledge, and have learned the remorse that comes with placing your own will in front of the will of God, you must leave the garden of Eden. But remember this, I will travel with you and with your flock, and with your off-spring for now and forever."

Jay looked up at Chris quizzically. "That's not how the chapter ends," he said. "Adam blamed Eve, and Eve blamed the snake. They were punished because of what they did. Eve and all women were cursed with the pain of bearing children, and Adam and all men were cursed with hard work and would only be able to survive through 'painful toil.'

"Maybe if they had shown remorse and been sorry for what they did, things would have been different," said Jay.

"Ah, now you're beginning to catch on." Chris replied. "In the world you're now in, things were different, and the end results were very different. Evil still exits, but in this world the remorse which followed the original sin was more dominant than in the world from which you came. The balance of good versus evil was swayed toward the good, as man in this world finds that the regret that he feels following an evil action is not worth the short-lived immediate gratification that caused that action."

Jay turned to look Chris directly in the eye. "Are you telling me that the story of Adam and Eve is not simply symbolic, that it is actually the true story of creation? And that now I'm in some sort of parallel world that is the same as the one that I left except that the history of man has been altered from the onset because of a different story of Adam and Eve?"

"Jay, what difference does it make if the story is

symbolic or the actual truth word for word? The point is man's relationship with God. In your world, man recognized right and wrong, good and evil. Every man had knowledge of God's will inside himself with an internal recognition of morality that existed but was frequently ignored. It was the nature of man to respond to his baser instincts, taking what he wanted, without concern, regret, or remorse, ultimately blaming others; both other men as well as an internal Satan for causing the evil actions that were in fact his responsibility. Man's will refused to suborn itself to God's will.

"In this parallel dimension, right from the beginning man had the same knowledge and ability to distinguish right from wrong, but man never lost sight of the fact that his very existence was possible by the grace of God. Man in this world is not perfect, and like Adam and Eve, often fails to live up to God's expectations. Yet, in this world, man has immediate awareness and recognition of his shortcomings, and feeling remorse, begs forgiveness, and continues to grow within God's Grace.

"No, it makes no difference if the story of Adam and Eve is factual or symbolic. The important thing is what the story represents. The type of humanity that grew and prospered in this world versus the mankind which labored and toiled for naught in the world from which you came."

Jay was beginning to understand the incomprehensible. That apparently slight change in the nature of man with an augmented sense of remorse and a diminished sense of pride had made an enormous difference in the outcome, and had changed the course of history.

Man still had free will, but more compassion. Pride and self esteem were there, but when they infringed upon the rights of others, then God-given empathy and a sense of brotherhood would intervene. Ego and love of self were equaled by love of God and by extension, love of fellow man. This was not a sinless Utopia, but when man erred, his nature was to ask for forgiveness rather than to hide or to place blame elsewhere.

Chris smiled when he saw that Jay had finally realized that now this world was the reality, and the previous world was no more than a memory, a memory that existed only in Jay's head.

This new world of love, understanding and forgiveness was the type of world that Jay had envisioned as the fulfillment of Chris' challenge of long ago, and now it was here. Jay was awe struck and speechless. Just as Chris had promised 70 years ago, if mankind failed to overcome evil, then mankind would cease to exist. The prophecy had come true, but in a way that Jay had never imagined.

Just then a sudden cloud burst hit the airport with a spectacular display of lightning, thunder and heavenly pyrotechnics. Just as suddenly, the sun burst through the clouds.

"My God, look at that incredible rainbow!" Someone in the hallway just outside the chapel was looking out over the airfield through the large windows and was struck by the sheer size and beauty of the colorful arc that had appeared.

Jay himself was momentarily mesmerized by the rainbow whose prismatic manifestation appeared to engulf the entire airport. He looked back to where Chris had been sitting and realized that Chris was gone. Then as he looked back at the rainbow, he knew that Chris wasn't really gone. He was still there with him as he had always been, now and forever.

Revelations 21:1 . . . 3-4

"Then I saw a new heaven and a new earth, for the first heaven and the first earth had passed away . . . Now the dwelling of God is with men, and He will live with them. They will be His people, and God Himself will be with them and be their God. He will wipe every tear from their eyes. There will be no more death or mourning or crying or pain, for the old order of things has passed away."

THE END